Sure Thing

Sure Thing

JANA ASTON

Edited by RJ Locksley
Cover Design by Kari March
Cover Photo by Sara Eirew
Formatting by Erik Gevers

CHAPTER ONE

Violet

I can do this.

Daisy does it. She does it all the time. I mean, I don't want to insinuate that my sister is the slutty one, but she's the slutty one.

I flick my eyes back across the hotel bar and hold the stranger's gaze. Three seconds. For three long agonizing seconds I lock eyes with him, then I smile and glance away. I got this tip from a women's magazine. The article was titled something like 'How to Snag Any Man You Want in Twenty Minutes or Less.' The three-second gaze and smile was tip number two. Tip number three is holding his gaze while licking my lips. I think that's beyond my capabilities though. That's mid-level seduction stuff and I'm definitely a beginner.

Tip number one was a glance while I touched my hair. So dumb.

I did it anyway.

Desperate times and all that.

But if tip number two fails I'm heading back to my room. Alone. Wait, I wonder if those tips were meant to be used simultaneously? Like, was I supposed to hold his gaze for three seconds, smile and touch my hair at the same time? I might have fucked this up. Which, whatever. I mean, how could this possibly work? As if all it would

1

take to get a hot stranger to have sex with me is three seconds of eye contact across a hotel bar? How does that even work?

Daisy would know.

Sometimes I hate the way she always knows, as if she's lived a lot longer than I have when she most certainly has not.

I sigh as I eye the maraschino cherry sunk in the last half-inch of my drink. I wonder if I tip the glass back if I can get to it, or if it'll just cling to the bottom and make me feel like an idiot.

Idiot, I decide.

I should get the check and go. I have a big week ahead of me. A great, big, almost-certain-to-be-disastrous week. I should be getting a good night's sleep, not practicing seduction techniques I picked up from an old magazine I found under my sister's couch. But as I lift my head to ask for the check a fresh drink is placed in front of me.

"From the guy in the blue shirt," the bartender tells me with a look back in his direction. She smiles at me and raises her brow in approval before bouncing off to someone calling for a refill.

Holy shit, that worked? The three-second gaze and smile actually worked? My eyes widen and I peek across the bar at the man and then down to the drink. What the hell was I thinking? What am I supposed to do now? I really should have read the rest of that article.

"Mind if I join you?"

I look up and he's standing beside my seat, a drink in his hand that he uses to signal towards the empty seat beside me. And what was that? Did I detect an accent? I think I did, but I can't be that lucky. I swallow my nerves and quickly run my eyes over him. Tall. Fit. Oxford shirt untucked, paired with a worn pair of jeans. Leather loafers on his feet and the hint of end-of-day scruff on his jaw. Thick, neatly cut, well-styled dark hair and expressive brown eyes watching me with interest.

"I hope the drink is to your satisfaction." He dips his head towards my beverage. "I asked the bartender to refresh you, but if you wanted something different..." He trails off with a small frown at my glass.

Oh.

My.

God.

Accent confirmed. I have just hit the holy grail of potential one-night stands.

"You're British," I say, fighting the grin from my face.

"I'll take that as a yes," he replies and sets his own drink on the bar top while resting on the stool beside me, his long legs bent slightly at the knees in order for his feet to rest on the floor. "Unless you have a problem with my country?" he inquires, brow raised and a small smile on his lips.

Do you know what's great about British men?

Everything.

I mean, I've never met one before this and they're likely no different than American men, but the accent. It's everything, right? You can say it's a cliché or whatever, but come on. It's panty-meltingly good. I know he's speaking the same language but the words just sound so much better falling from his lips.

"I'm Jennings," he says, extending a hand, and I almost laugh. Jennings? It's obviously fake. This guy is too old to have a trendy millennial name like Jennings. Also, it sounds British for 'I'm giving you a fake name.' But fine, I'm game.

"Rose," I tell him and slip my hand into his. His hand engulfs mine and he's not quick to withdraw, instead running his thumb gently over the back of my hand. I like the feeling a lot, the texture and warmth of his skin creating an immediate spark of interest in touching a whole lot more of him.

"Rose," he repeats, pausing and tilting his head a fraction as if he doesn't believe me. He shouldn't, it's not my name. But it's close enough and he didn't give me his real name, so it's all he's getting. I'm not supposed to be here right now anyway, so Rose it is.

"Rose," I confirm. "And no, I don't have any issues with your country." I smile and linger on his face for a moment. I'm actually a bit of an Anglophile, truth be told. When Will and Kate got married I woke up early to watch the wedding live and I've binge-watched all six seasons of *Downton Abbey*. Twice. And while I've never had afternoon tea I'm positive it'd be just my thing. "Thank you for the drink," I add, picking my glass up.

"You're welcome. What exactly is it that you're drinking?" he asks, eyeing my glass again as he takes a sip from his own. I'd guess he's drinking bourbon, the amber liquid swaying in his glass over a single ice cube. It looks expensive, if I could judge the cost of his drink based on seeing an inch of it swirling in a glass. It must be the British accent that makes him seem posh inside of a nondescript Sheraton by the airport.

"A champagne cocktail," I reply with a blush. It's a stupid drink, but I like it.

"Ahh," he replies, and even that half a word sounds better in his accent. "Is that a popular drink in this country?"

It's not.

But wait, he doesn't know that, does he?

"Very." I nod. Wow. Who knew I was such a great liar? This week might be easier than I thought. "So what brings you to Washington?" I ask, changing the subject. I run my fingertip around the rim of my glass and wonder if I can really do this. It's a great opportunity though, isn't it? He's perfect, appears interested and I'll never see him again. If I'm going to get back on the horse I couldn't ask for a better scenario. Or a better horse. Like a totally-out-of-my-league thoroughbred kind of horse I'd most definitely like to ride.

"Business," he replies. "You?"

"Same," I reply quickly and wave the question off with my hand. "Dull," I add with a smile and a roll of my eyes.

"It was dull, yes," he says in agreement, his gaze direct before dropping his eyes to my lips.

I feel a flush moving down my neck and I swallow.

"So you're in town for a fortnight or something?"

"Have you any idea what a fortnight is, Rose?" He laughs and takes a sip from his glass as he watches me.

"Um, four nights?" I guess. I don't actually have a clue what a fortnight is but I like the way it sounds and I've never had the opportunity to use it in conversation.

"A fortnight is two weeks, and no, I won't be in America quite that long."

Perfect.

I smile and drop my eyes to look for a ring. I may be willing to use him to get my groove back, but I'm not willing to enable a cheater.

"And what about you, Rose? Where is home for you when you're not staying at this hotel?"

Sore subject. "Here and there." My sister's couch, but I don't say that. I'm way too old to be in between apartments. And jobs. So I definitely don't tell him any of that. Instead I smile before taking a large gulp of my drink. This week is all about bluffing anyway.

"Here and there?" he questions with a raised brow and

tilt of his head. Great. He probably thinks I'm not stable enough for a one-night stand. I need to redirect this conversation.

"Where did you say you lived?" I ask. "London?" I add as a guess because, yes, my geography skills are so stellar that London is the only city in England that I can come up with quickly.

"London, yes," he agrees while watching me. "In Mayfair. Hertford Street," he adds. I'm fairly certain he's being specific to make a point about me being so vague. Too bad.

"Sounds nice."

"Does it?" He smiles at me like I'm amusing him. I take another sip of my drink and eye the cherry at the bottom of my glass. The last one got away from me when the waitress replaced my drink with the one Jennings sent.

"I like your shirt," I offer. Subject change, take two. "Is it bespoke?"

"Shall I ask if you know what 'bespoke' means or is it just another British term you've been anxious to use?" He shakes his head this time when he laughs.

"It means fancy?" I ask, because he's correct. I don't know what that word means either.

"It means custom-made. And no"—he pauses as he glances down at his shirt—"this shirt is not bespoke." The pause makes me wonder if his other shirts are custom. He does seem a little fancy, but who has custom dress shirts made? No one I know, that's for sure.

I'm distracted when a gaggle of what appears to be a traveling soccer team of pre-teens moves through the lobby towards the elevators. Excited calls about who is rooming with who and snippets about meeting at the hotel pool echo through the lobby as they pass.

"It's getting kind of loud in here," I say, glancing towards the lobby entrance where the kids have already passed. It's not, not really. But seriously, how do I move this from drinks to sex? How?

"Hmm," he murmurs, his eyes on me.

"Do you want to go somewhere a little quieter?" I suggest.

He pauses, glass halfway to his lips, and looks at me in surprise. I must really suck at this. Is my sister right? Ugh. It pains me to even think it. Lord help me if I ever have to admit it out loud. My sister is rarely right, but she might be this time. I might be incapable of pulling this off.

"Cutting right to the chase, are we?" he questions, a small smirk on his lips. "I had you pegged for another two rounds of hemming and hawing before you were up for it."

Up for it? Does that mean sex? I eye the cherry in my glass again then force myself to look him directly in the eyes. I hold his gaze for three seconds before I speak. It worked the first time, right?

"Look, I'm a sure thing," I tell him with a small shrug while shifting my eyes away then back.

"Are you?" The amusement on his face is clear.

No. I'm not a sure thing. I've never been a sure thing. But I've never been Rose before either, so to hell with it—tonight I am.

"Yup," I say with more confidence than I feel.

"Hmm," he says again and so help me, his murmur is the sexiest freaking thing ever. He tilts my glass and reaches inside with a single long finger, pulling the cherry to the rim. Extracting it, he holds it to my lips and I open my mouth and take it from him, my tongue sliding under his fingers as I pull the sweetened fruit from his grip. I roll it across my tongue and look into his eyes, wondering what's next.

"Well, let's go then, shall we?"

Oh, shit. I swallow the cherry and worry for a second that it's going to stick in my throat and I'll choke. Did I really just tell a complete stranger I'm a sure thing?

CHAPTER TWO

Jennings

She's lying, this girl. I'm not sure what she's lying about—her name for starters, who knows what else. Not that it matters. I don't really give a toss, do I? She's a distraction, nothing more, a very welcome and unexpected distraction before the beginning of a dull but hopefully informative week.

A sure thing, she said. I stifle a chuckle as I hit the lift call button and add that to her list of lies. I sent her the drink after I caught her looking at me in the bar but I didn't expect it to lead anywhere. I expected, based on her shy smiles, that she was interested enough to allow me to sit with her. Pass an hour or two in conversation before she demurely excused herself with talk of an early morning. When she sucked in a breath and made the comment about moving to a quieter location, she surprised me. When I tilted my head in question and she blurted out, "I'm a sure thing"—well, fuck me.

"Rose," I say as the lift doors open. There's no response, her head buried in her phone as she attempts to discreetly tap out a text. If I had to guess I'd say she's sending a safety check to a friend. Ensuring her phone GPS is on. She likely snapped a photo of me when I wasn't paying attention and sent that too.

She's cute.

"Rose," I repeat while laying a hand on her arm. She looks momentarily confused, a flash so brief I wouldn't have noticed if I hadn't been looking for it. She's definitely not called Rose.

She smiles and precedes me into the lift as I wonder what brought her here, to this hotel and to this moment. Boredom? A bad breakup? Trying to prove to herself that she's desirable?

I'm happy to help with that.

But I can't call her Rose. When she remembers this night it shouldn't be with another woman's name on my lips. And she will remember this night.

The lift doors close and I turn to her. She's wearing a short-sleeve shirt, her breasts forming an exquisite curve under the material. I run the tip of my finger down her bare arm and watch her nipples harden as her eyes move to mine, then to the lift control panel and back again.

"Are you suggesting we have sex in this elevator? Because if you're fast enough to come before those doors open again, I'm not actually interested." Her brow creases and her face is a mixture of regret and arousal. This time I do laugh as I reach past her and hit the button for three.

"No, love. I wasn't suggesting a romp in the lift," I assure her and move closer without touching her. Her pupils widen and her chest rises as she sucks in a breath and tilts her head back to meet my gaze. She's wearing a knee-length skirt and heeled sandals on her feet. The skirt flows and would easily accommodate the spread of her legs if I were to boost her off her feet and wrap them around my hips. It's a tempting thought, and she's slight enough that she'd be easy to pick up and fuck against a wall. But no, that's not in my plans for her tonight. I can definitely spare her more than a few minutes of my time.

The floor beneath us jolts the slightest bit, signaling

the lift doors are about to open. I keep my eyes on hers as the doors slide and then lean past her to place a hand against the open lift door, blocking it from closing. "After you," I tell her, my voice low. She pivots and exits, stopping as her eyes rest on the opposite wall where an arrow points in one direction for rooms three hundred to three-nineteen and another for rooms three-twenty to three-forty. She pauses and I wonder if this just became too real for her. I wonder if she'll back out.

I take her hand and lead her to the right. She follows, her hand soft in mine, her heeled footsteps near silent on the hotel carpet. I wave the keycard to my room in front of the electronic lock and push the door open when the light flashes green, stretching my arm out and holding it open for her. She drops my hand and walks into the room and I note how lovely her hair is. Long tumbling waves of rich chestnut brown or possibly black resting against her back. It will look even better on my pillow.

She stops a few feet into the room and looks back at me over her shoulder as the door snaps shut behind me. Seeing her here in my room, I feel a moment of regret. Because while I know nothing about her, I know she deserves more than this hotel. Not that there's anything wrong with it. It's perfectly nice, in a business-class, family vacation sort of way. But I'd prefer if I had her in a five-star with a view of the capital, the lights of the city casting a soft glow through the room. A marble bathroom with a shower big enough for two. But we're here, so the view of a fast-food chain across the street will have to do.

All she has with her is a small bag that can't fit much more than a mobile phone and currency. I watch her set it down on the sideboard across from the bed then turn to me, a tiny lift of her chin as she likely reminds herself why she's here, a mental pep talk flashing across her face. Then she wets her lips and smiles, but it's for her, not me.

She has absolutely no idea how to proceed, does she? I've bedded virgins more aggressive than this woman.

"So how do you want to do this?" I ask her as I close the distance between us, my hands in my pockets and my steps unhurried. I stop before her and when she doesn't move I untuck my hands and trail one finger along the shell of her ear. She bites her bottom lip between her teeth.

"Naked," she replies earnestly, flicking her eyes from mine to my chest. "I'd like to do it naked."

I'm definitely keeping her all night.

"Take these off," I tell her, with a gentle tap of a finger to an earring. She removes them from both ears and places them next to her tiny bag, then looks back to me expectantly.

"How do you want to fuck?" I ask and pick up her hand. I kiss the inside of her wrist and meet her eyes. "Soft or hard? Fast or slow? Dirty or dirty?"

"Um…" She blinks, her skin flushed. "Yes."

I'm not sure she's even processed what I've asked, but I'm certain I had the answer before the door closed anyhow. And I wasn't asking for any particular reason other than to watch her response. She's not aggressive, this girl, she'd love it if I took the reins, so to speak. Removed whatever doubts she has in her mind about her desirability by leaving no question of my interest. And I'm interested. Interested in fucking her in every position possible until she passes out, exhausted and sated. I drop her wrist and rub my bottom lip with my thumb while I enjoy that visual for a moment.

"Your blouse," I say, my tone brooking no argument,

not that I'm expecting one. "Take it off."

"Okay. And you take off your pants," she responds in complete sincerity, her tongue peeking out between her lips. Her fingers have already moved to one of the buttons fastening her blouse as her gaze drops to my cock.

I swell in response. Hell, I was hard for her before I knew she was game. Her blouse hits the floor as I unbuckle my belt and unsnap my jeans before moving to my shirt and unbuttoning from the bottom up. Her hands pause for the briefest of moments before she reaches behind her and unzips what must have been a hidden zipper on her skirt. It pools around her feet and she steps out of the circle of fabric, leaving her sandals behind, then looks down with a tiny grimace before scooping her clothing off the floor and placing it quickly next to her earrings and bag.

She squares her shoulders as she turns back to face me, naked save for a pretty bra and pants set. Cotton, I'd guess, with delicate lace trim. Sweet. She's sweet. And I wonder again what brought her to me tonight. I wonder if someone's hurt her, but the idea of someone cheating on her seems ludicrous, as does me having that thought when I've known her only an hour. Actually, not even that. I don't know her at all. I've not even kissed her yet. Why does she want this? Why now?

I drop my shirt to the floor and leave it there. My trousers follow suit and she glances at the pile of clothing for a brief moment, her fingers twitching. I think she's contemplating picking my clothing off the floor like she did her own but she refrains with a slight shake of her head, then turns her attention to my bare chest with a smile. A feisty little grin that she must feel isn't very sophisticated because she immediately tries to hide it.

"So," she says with a small shrug as she places her palm on my chest, her fingers spreading outwards in exploration. The slight inhale of breath and bubbly grin tell me she's happy with her choice for a one-off, gaining confidence in the moment. She presses her lips together to hide the smile then asks, "Now what?" Her head tilts towards the side as she asks, the hint of her pink tongue pressing between her lips. I can find a better use for that, most certainly.

That's it. I'm not waiting any longer. I wrap my fingers behind her neck and yank her to me as I cover her lips with my own. Her lips are soft and warm and she tastes faintly like the cherry she sucked off my fingers earlier and smells of vanilla or possibly coconut. I think it's her hair. And then she moans, the most delightful microscopic moan of excitement or approval. I like it, whatever it is. I dig my fingers into her hair as I maneuver her to deepen the kiss and it's every bit as silky as I'd imagined. Thick, silky strands that feel seductive under my fingers. Strands I could hold like a leash while I fuck her from behind or while she kneels before me with my cock in her mouth.

I lift her off her feet, her legs wrapping around my waist as I walk her towards the bed, unsnapping her bra as I go. Her arms are crossed behind my neck, her fingers working their way into the hair at my nape as she breaks away from my mouth, moving her lips to my jaw and grinding her pelvis against me with a subtle lift of her hips. I set her on the edge of the bed and slide the straps of her bra down her arms till it's dangling from my fingertips, then toss it aside. Her right shoulder hitches a fraction but her eyes don't follow the bra so I don't think she's contemplating picking it up off the floor. Instead her eyes rest on my chest and she quickly bites her bottom lip before releasing it again. What is she thinking and why do I care? She's hot and she wants me, end of.

"I didn't expect you, Rose, but I'm glad you're here. On my bed. Ready for me."

She looks uncertain for a moment, as if she's second-guessing her decision, and I wonder how experienced she is. If I should be worried about her being underage. It's doubtful but worth asking. I've always subscribed to the 'ask, don't guess' policy when it comes to women.

"How old are you, love?" I question and her eyes snap up from my chest to meet mine.

"Twenty-six," she answers immediately, and she no longer looks uncertain, she looks irked. "How old are you?"

"I'm thirty-six." I smile. I like her. I can't imagine she gives a toss what my age is. I think she only spat the question out as some form of retaliation for asking hers.

"Thirty-six?" Her brows rise and she gives me a quick once-over before shrugging and working to clear her face of surprise. "Right, okay. I guess that's fine."

I raise a brow at her. Is this girl I'm never going to see again really giving me shit about my age?

She runs her eyes across my chest again and then tilts her head to the side with a, "Huh," said to herself. Then she twists her lips before meeting my eyes again with a, "Yeah, okay." I can't recall ever knowing a woman so transparent with her thoughts. I find myself smiling again, amused with her.

I roll her nipple between my fingers and she inhales. Her reactions are stunning. Time to get this liaison back on track. I kneel on the floor in front of her, hook my thumbs into the sides of her knickers and pull until she lifts her hips enough for me to slide the material over her bottom and to the floor. Her toenails are painted hot pink and I slide my hands along the arches of her feet as I go about admiring how lovely she is. The soft arch of her hips, the shape of her calves, delicate ankles and a tiny birthmark on the top of her left foot.

I slide her knees apart and move between them, her thighs spread wide. Her breath catches as I grasp a nipple with my teeth and lightly pull. Her tits are as perfect as every other part of her, but they're not my focus right now. I want to taste her—no, I need to taste her. I need the memory of her taste on my tongue when I think of this night or I'll always wonder what I missed.

I push her back onto the bed and work my way down her stomach, my destination clear. Her legs flutter against my shoulders as if she's tensed, but then they relax and fall further open as one of those delightful half-sighs, half-moans I've already come to associate with her emits from her lips.

I spread her apart with my thumbs and now I'm thankful for the light, neon or otherwise, peeking into the room from the street. Lovely. She's so fucking lovely. She's completely smooth and I want to cover every inch of her with my mouth, my tongue. She's already wet and I've barely touched her, her arousal glistening at me like a dirty gift.

I place my tongue on her and run it slowly from top to bottom. By the time I pull her clit between my lips her hands are in my hair. Within another minute she's got one foot flat on the bed for leverage while the heel of her other foot is pressing into my back.

Her enthusiasm is irresistible, her scent intoxicating. She really is a gift I wasn't expecting tonight.

I slip a finger into her and she moans something about Jesus. That won't do.

"Jennings," I remind her. Her eyes are glazed and it

takes her a moment to focus on the fact that my tongue is being used for talking instead of where she wants it.

"Right." She blinks. "Right, I didn't forget. I can call you Jennings, sure."

She's an odd little duck. A cute vixen with a dash of sexy and I want more. God, I want her. I keep my eyes on her as I slip my finger back into her wet heat. I love the feel of the inside of a woman—the warmth and texture, the slickness of her lubrication. I miss the feel of a woman bare against my cock with nothing between us. Fuck, it's been forever since I've felt that. Not that I'll be feeling it tonight either. I'm not an idiot.

But when I suck her clit between my lips again while pressing two fingers on that tiny bundle of nerves inside of her and she screams my name, I sort of wish I was.

CHAPTER THREE

Violet

Oh, holy hell.

That thing he just did was like a public service—a public service that should be open to all women, everywhere. Regardless of political party, race, religion or border. It should be law or something, I think with a laugh as I throw an arm over my eyes. I wonder what else this guy can do? How did he know how to get me off so quickly? We're not even done yet and this has to be the best one-night stand in the history of sex. I can't believe this is my life right now!

"Is something funny, love?" he asks as he stands and picks up his pants, retrieving a condom from his wallet before tossing them on the floor again. The skin around his eyes creases in a way that makes me think he's amused, not hurt, by my laughter.

"No, nothing's funny," I reply, but I can't keep the grin off my face.

I scoot back on the bed until my head is on the pillows. Then I remember that investigative news special I saw about hotel room bedding and cringe. I think I'm lying on a duvet cover though, and surely they wash those? But just in case, I slip my legs underneath and then flip the cover back and push it to the end of the bed.

The guy—Jennings—pauses with a small smile on his

face, watching me. Whatever. Germs are no joke. I lean against the headboard and smile back at him. "So what else you got?" I ask and—what the hell—I run my eyes over him from head to toe. He's still got his underwear on so I can't check out everything, but I like everything I can see, that's for sure. Broad shoulders. Impressive abs—how the heck is he almost forty? Narrow waist. Strong legs. Impressive bulge. What? Like I didn't linger a moment there during my perusal? I pat the bed next to me with my palm and grin.

"What else have I got?" He laughs and tosses the condom on the nightstand before gripping my ankle and dragging me down the bed until I'm horizontal. I yelp in surprise before sucking in a breath as he lowers himself over me, holding himself above me with his arms. Then he kisses me and I groan. I can faintly taste myself on him and it makes me wet all over again. This man. His mouth. He's... carnal and I love it. Maybe it's a British thing? Maybe they're all super-amazing in bed? I've never been with a man from another country before so I don't have a comparison. All I know is tonight was a really good decision.

His accent is going to be the death of me. In the best way. I'm glad he's not calling me Rose right now. I wish he knew my name. Hearing Violet on his tongue... And the way he keeps calling me "love"—it's so British of him, right? And it works for me—like a lot.

His magic mouth skills do not disappoint in the kissing department either. It should be awkward, kissing a stranger. It sounds stupid considering what he just did with his mouth. That I'd even give a second thought to the intimacy of kissing mouth to mouth. Kissing is so filled with breathing and saliva, taste and tongues and angles and pressure and Mr. Mouth here is good at all of it. His lips move from mine to my jaw as I tangle my fingers into his hair. He sucks my earlobe between his teeth as the tiniest huff of breath in my ear makes me shiver before his tongue wets that spot just behind my ear, causing me to press my pelvis against him, desperate for more.

More of this, more of that, more of whatever he's got to offer.

His mouth is on mine again and I moan when he drops his arms enough for my nipples to rub against his chest. When his tongue presses into my mouth and tangles with my own. When he nips at my lip and kisses his way down my throat. By the time he moves lower and cups the underside of my breast with one hand while flicking his thumb over the nipple, I'm ready to beg. Instead I swear at him.

"Fuck... Jennings." I moan and arch my back when he flattens his tongue across the surface of my breast and flicks his thumb back and forth over my nipple again. That fucking mouth of his.

I need him inside of me. I can't remember the last time I was this anxious to move from foreplay to penetration. When it didn't feel like a cursory few kisses were delivered before the guy was whipping out his dick and grunting like he was fucking with way more skill than he had.

Like sometimes my ex Mark liked to bark, "Take it, take it," while he thrust aggressively and I'd mumble something like, "Hmmm, yeah," while I'd snake my hand down to rub my clit and think, *Take what?* Take what exactly? Because it mostly just felt like he was bouncing me on the bed and poking at me with a super-plus tampon while he played alpha man. And I am not saying this from a place of bitter ex-girlfriend. His penis was perfectly normal-sized. It's just that some men have a really overinflated opinion of the skill they have with their average-sized penises. That's all.

I'm positive that whatever Magic Mouth is packing under those cotton briefs he will use it with skill. He seems pretty skilled. Maybe being almost forty has its benefits? God, I hope he's still got stamina though. Don't men lose stamina as they age? *Don't let me down, Jennings,* I think as I slide my hands down to his briefs and push them over his hips, my intent clear. *Do not let me down. You are my first one-night stand, don't be my last. Don't be the reason I give up entirely and take up knitting and invest in a vibrator collection. Don't be—*

Never mind.

I've got his briefs past his ass. His cock just thumped onto my stomach. Like, if my stomach was capable of emitting a grunt from the contact, it would. Hell, yes. Keep calm and carry on. God save the Queen. Think of England. I let a giggle loose as he reaches for the condom.

"You're a very odd sort of girl, aren't you?" he asks, but he's smiling again, a lazy lust-fueled smile that reaches his eyes. He has nice eyes.

"I'm usually the sensible one," I murmur. Throwing caution to the wind has never been my thing, but I think it's going to be. Why not, right? It's not like I have an apartment or a job to lose. They're already gone, might as well embrace it. Seize the day, carpe diem. Easy, breezy me.

"The sensible what?" he asks as he tears the condom wrapper with his teeth. Why is that sexy? I should probably get out more if that move is enough to do it for me.

"Nothing," I reply. "Never mind," I add while sliding

one of my knees up to plant my foot on the bed next to his thigh. He's slipped that condom on one-handed with practiced ease and settled both my legs outside of his on the bed. His weight rests on one arm as he uses the other to guide his cock, nudging at my entrance. He pushes just inside and it's already good. I've missed this, and I decide then and there that the new carefree me is going to put out more.

Then he slides in deeper and it's better than good.

He locks eyes with mine as he sinks all the way in. He groans and I suck in air. I wiggle my pelvis a little, adjusting to the feel of him while trapping my lower lip between my teeth, which he promptly removes with his own then kisses me.

I make a weird noise in my throat and rotate my hips towards him because he just feels so perfect. I clench around his cock and his eyes darken then close for a moment. When he opens them he grins and kisses me again before sliding back, almost out, then back in. He teases me with the most deliciously long, deliberate strokes. Deep then shallow. Receding then forging. When he pulls out to the tip I dig my fingertips into his shoulders, wanting him back. I'd beg him for it if he asked.

Instead he withdraws and moves to his knees, hooking my thighs under his forearms and pulling me to raise my bottom off the bed, then sliding back in. This time when he enters me it's fast and hard. I reach over my head and rest my hands against the headboard, both to stop myself from hitting it and to aid him in his task. Sex has never felt like this. Never.

"Oh, my God, don't stop."

"I'm not stopping, love. Not a chance."

His balls smack against me as he thrusts and it's so

lewd, the only sounds in the room skin slapping skin mingled with our breathing. It's wet and hot, hard and dirty and I want to come right now, but I want it to last longer too.

Spoiler: it lasts longer.

Magic Mouth is also some kind of orgasm genie because he seems to know exactly how to keep me on the brink of coming, leading me right up to the edge then backing away. It's agony.

"Please let me come," I whine. "Please, please, please."

"You are quite the delightful little surprise, love," he responds as he rolls us over so I'm on top.

"I am?" I gasp. This new position is unexpected and I pause for a moment. I don't really like to be on top.

"You are." He cocks an eyebrow and taps my hip, indicating the ball is in my court.

I usually feel conspicuous on top. Exposed. But fuck it, I'm never going to see this guy again and I want to come. And I am in control up here. Plus, the way he looks at me is exhilarating. Like my tits aren't too small and my stomach doesn't look pudgy from that angle. No, I see nothing but lustful attentiveness in his eyes. I run my eyes over his chest again and lift up on my thighs just a little and slide back down onto him. He really does have a nice chest. Sculpted and toned with a smattering of chest hair that's hot, not unruly.

"Touch yourself," he commands and my eyes fly back to his. His hands have moved to my thighs, his fingers resting against my skin seductively.

I swallow and avert my eyes for a second, then look back to him as I move my hand to my clit. Then I rub two fingers over myself while setting the pace on his cock. Rocking back and forth, in and out. He watches me intently and when his eyes drop to where we're joined my fingers still for a moment until he says, "Don't stop," his voice low and seductive, lids low, a groan coming from his chest. So I keep going, emboldened. His lust is encouraging. Empowering. I pick up the pace on his cock and with my fingers until I come.

It sneaks up on me, fast and hard. I drop my head forward, my hands braced on his chest for balance. He stills deep inside of me while I spasm around his cock, his hands on my hips holding me tight until the pulsing slows, and then he's hammering into me from below, his own orgasm following with a ragged, "Fuck, love," passing his lips as his eyes close, his head tilted back in ecstasy. His jaw tightens along with his grip on my thighs when he comes and I think he's beautiful. I catalog his features in my memory before collapsing on his chest.

That was perfect.

The perfect one-night stand.

CHAPTER FOUR

Jennings

Bloody hell, last night was unforeseen. The American girl was something, I muse as I wipe the remnants of shaving cream from my jaw. I wonder if I should have gotten her number? But no, I'm only in Washington for another day before I have to board a godforsaken bus and play happy tourist. Besides, I never even got her real name—surely she wasn't giving me her number.

Anyway, she left without saying anything. Looked at the clock this morning and bolted out of bed. Dressed and was out the door within a minute. "Thank you!" she chirped with her hand on the door, her body already halfway into the hall. "It was nice meeting you!" she added as she released the door and disappeared from sight.

It was very nice meeting you, love. Not sure I've ever heard it phrased quite that way the morning after, but very nice indeed.

I love women. I love taking them to dinner. Walking them to their door. Caressing their cheeks as I cup their jaws and kiss them before they invite me inside. Most of all, I love fucking them. I love discovering what gets them wet. What causes their breath to hitch and their toes to curl. What combination of moves will make a woman scream my name and come all over my cock.

Rose—or whatever her name is—is not what I'm here for, not at all. But she made me laugh. The way she lied about her name as if having an assignation with a stranger is a covert mission. Perhaps it was for her, but it still made me smile. And the way her eyes lit up when she asked if I was British, fuck. Later she asked me to "say something British" to her while we lay naked on the bed.

I shake my head and laugh out loud at the memory. And that ridiculous champagne cocktail she was drinking. Another lie. That drink isn't hip in any country. And I can't recall the last time a woman ditched me after sex.

Perhaps I'll find her in the hotel bar again tonight. Maybe. Do I want to? I don't normally look for a redo, but I wouldn't pass on another night with that girl.

Why the hell did I let her run off this morning? She caught me off guard with her exit; I was still blissed out on sex, and catching up on the change in time zones. And then she was gone, the scent of coconut gone with her while I committed the vision of her wide-eyed smile to memory. The look on her face when I made her come— multiple times. The vision of her hair spread across my pillow. The way she hesitated for a moment while astride me and then ran her fingertip down my chest before flattening both palms against me and rocking herself to another orgasm.

I'm hopeful fate will be in my favor for another round with her.

But first: Nan. I'm here for Nan, I remind myself.

I finish dressing. Jeans and a t-shirt will suffice for today. I find my wallet on the floor with yesterday's clothing and pocket it, dumping the clothing on top of my suitcase so housekeeping doesn't trip over it. I glance at my watch and see I've got just enough time to make it to the lobby to meet Nan. Our guided tour of American historic sites this week didn't include a stop at the National Gallery and she mentioned she'd be quite chuffed to go there, so off we go. Lord help me. Art's not really my thing, but for Nan I'll go along.

I groan at the thought of all the work I'll be missing this week. I do not have time for tourism, but it's my turn so I'll make the time. I'll figure it out. Besides, I have my laptop. Certainly I'll be able to get some work done while the bus is transporting us from city to city so I can keep abreast of business in the UK.

I exit the lift at the lobby and make a cursory sweep of the bar with a quick glance. Not that I expect to see the girl sitting there at ten in the morning, but doesn't hurt to look, does it?

Nan is waiting for me at the lobby entrance and I wrap my arm around her, her scent as familiar as England itself. Then I push the girl from last night out of my mind and focus on the reason I'm here.

CHAPTER FIVE

Violet

This is the worst idea Daisy has ever had. And trust me, over the years she's had some bad ideas. When we were five she insisted we were allowed to paint our own nails, ending in our parents replacing the carpet in our bedroom. When we were ten she told me she didn't need to study for a math test because our brains were linked and since I knew the answers she would too. When we were thirteen she convinced me to switch clothes with her in the bathroom during lunch before afternoon classes—and take her science exam for her. We pulled it off but I was a nervous wreck, sure we'd be caught and tossed into kid jail. When we were sixteen she impersonated me and flirted with a guy I was too shy to flirt with myself. She got him to ask her, pretending to be me, on a date. So technically he was asking me. I think. Anyway, I was the one who went on the actual date—and I had my first kiss with that guy, so I guess the plan wasn't a total fail.

Following rules is my jam. Breaking them is Daisy's.

So why did I go along with this?

This is sheer lunacy.

I'm twenty-six years old. Way too old to be doing what is essentially a twin switcheroo. I pull out my phone and call Daisy while eyeing the Sutton Travel tour bus sitting in front of the Sheraton.

"I can't do this," I tell her as soon as she picks up.

She sighs into my ear. "I'm so tired of your bullshit, Violet. Pull on your big-girl panties and just do it." That's my sister for you.

"Thanks, Daisy. That's a very nice thing to say."

"You're welcome. Look, no one is forcing you to do this. If you want to go back to my place and sulk on the couch for another six months you're welcome to it. In fact, take my room. I'm not home anyway."

I sigh into the phone.

"Exactly, Vi. What you need is a kick in the ass. An adventure!" Her voice lifts on 'adventure' and I know she's about to ramp up her sales pitch. "Aren't you bored, Violet? You should live a little. Throw caution to the wind. Grab life by the balls!" She's likely waving her arms around as she says this, knowing my sister. "You're always the responsible one and really, where has it gotten you? Nowhere," she adds unnecessarily. Because it's true. I've always been the planner and yet here I am, jobless and living on her sofa.

I take a moment to feel smug about the secret one-night stand I had last night. Daisy doesn't know about that, does she? Nope. And that was super-unplanned. It was a spontaneous home run, if I do say so myself, and I know I'm smiling like an idiot as I recall last night. I don't have another one-night stand to compare it to, but I'm fairly certain it was exceptional. I still can't believe I went through with it, it's so not my thing to hook up with a stranger. I've never even come close to hooking up with a stranger before. I totally nailed the one-night stand thing. Pun intended.

I wonder if I might find him again tonight in the hotel bar or if he's already checked out? Of course, if I sleep with him again it wouldn't technically be a one-night stand anymore, would it?

"Hello, Violet? Are you listening to me?" Daisy interrupts my smutty reminiscing and I snap to attention.

"Yes, I'm listening." I've really turned into a liar in the last twenty-four hours, haven't I?

"So it's no biggie, Vi. Do it or don't. Stay or go."

"It's no biggie? You'll get fired if I go home, Daisy. Because this tour starts in five minutes and you're not here. Where are you anyway? Are you in an airport? It sounds like you're in an airport. And how can you be so blasé about getting fired? Getting fired is a really big deal, Daisy." I would know.

"Getting fired is not that big a deal. I keep telling you that. Perspective, Vi. You're not homeless or hungry, and getting fired is not an ending, it's a beginning. A beginning to something bigger and better," she says in that dreamy way that only my sister can. "Life changes every single day. You never know what tomorrow is going to bring, believe me. Seize the fucking day."

"What is so urgent that you're willing to jeopardize this job anyway? It's a pretty sweet gig for you." Daisy's main focus is travel blogging, but these tours essentially allow her to double-dip. She gets paid for doing the tours and during her downtime takes photographs and searches out hidden gems a large tour group couldn't do, but which are perfect material for her blog. She's built her blog from nothing to making a good income from ads and affiliate links and she works for herself so it's easy to manage around her schedule with Sutton Travel. It's ideal and she'd be crazy to give it up.

"I've got a thing to do," she says breezily.

A thing. I'm not sure I even want to know.

"I'm hanging up now," she says. "Just get on the bus,

Violet. You can fake your way through this tour. You've seen me do it, it's not that complicated. And I gave you step-by-step notes."

"I'm gonna mess it up." I swallow in dread. "How can I possibly give a tour I've only been on once?" I did tag along on this same tour last month when it was undersold and she had a few empty seats on the bus. I wasn't really paying attention though. I spent most of that trip spying on Mark's Facebook page, which is idiotic. But at the time it felt so necessary.

"They don't know that, Violet. We've been over this. No one on that tour is going to know you don't know what you're doing. None of them are even American. You can tell them whatever you want. Just smile and make sure you don't lose anyone during a bathroom stop and you're golden."

"You're making the assumption that only Americans know American history?" I question her, for the tenth time. This idea is lunacy.

"I'm making the assumption that you don't have a job and you could use the paycheck that Sutton Travel is going to give me for this tour. Which I'll transfer to your account."

Touché.

But it's true. And I have zero interviews scheduled for this week. Nada. I've been sending résumés for six months and I've done nothing but go on interviews for positions I don't even want and don't get offered. Which just makes me feel like shit because I can't even turn down something I'm not interested in.

"And I know that you can follow the script I wrote well enough to fake your way past an assortment of tourists from other countries," she adds. "You're not an idiot. It's not like you're going to mistake the White

House for the Capitol Building. Just follow the cheat sheet I made for you."

"Just follow the cheat sheet," I repeat. It's ironic, since cheating got Daisy through most of high school.

"The bus driver has the route and all the stops are prearranged. You're handing the group over to local experts in Washington and Gettysburg. You're practically just dropping them off and picking them up. You got this."

"Right." I blow out a breath and eye the bus again. "And you haven't done any tours with this bus driver, right? Tom? He's not going to expect me to know him?"

"Nope. I told you there's at least a couple hundred drivers. I rarely saw the same one twice and I've never met this one. You're good."

"Okay," I mumble. "This is still a terrible idea."

"It's a genius idea," she replies, full of confidence. "Besides, if you don't show up all those tourists are going to be stranded."

"That's not true," I reply slowly, rolling my eyes even though she can't see me.

"It's sort of true. Your first airport pickup is in less than an hour. The company wouldn't be able to get a replacement there that quickly. Just think of all those nice Canadians standing at the airport check-in spot wondering where you are."

"You mean wondering where *you* are," I reply drily.

"Whatever. They'll be sad, Violet. Sad they came all the way to America and no one greeted them."

"Why are you singling out the Canadians anyway? Wouldn't everyone be sad?"

"I thought I'd pull on your heartstrings a little and everyone knows how nice the Canadians are," she says, unabashed. "I bet one of them offers you a maple candy before the week is up."

"You're ridiculous," I mutter, but I'm smiling.

"Love you, Vi. You're my peanut butter."

"And you're my jelly."

We end the call and I pin the Sutton Travel name badge with "Daisy" stamped on it to my top with renewed confidence. Daisy's right. I can do this. And I really do need the cash.

This is what happens when the company you work for is sold two weeks before you're due to close on a condo and your job is eliminated. It turns out that banks frown on giving thirty-year mortgages to people without jobs. I'd already given notice on my apartment, most of my possessions packed into boxes ready for my move, when my world imploded. The boxes moved into storage and I moved onto Daisy's couch.

I lost my boyfriend at the same time.

When I say I lost him I mean it literally. He's alive—I just don't have him anymore. Because we worked together. In different departments—nothing scandalous. He was the owner's son—everyone knew about us, it wasn't a secret and it didn't get me any special favors, of course not. I'd never have wanted special favors.

Except...

When it happened I was the last to know. The very last. I was running an errand on my lunch break when the email was sent notifying employees that we'd been sold to a larger company. A larger company that only needed half of the current staff. A larger company that was relocating Mark to another city in a high-level executive position—part of the deal when his father sold the company, of course. When I got back to the office a human resources representative from the new company was there to offer me a severance package.

Do you know what severance packages look like when you're twenty-six? A week's pay for every year of service. I'd been there for three and a half years. Three weeks of pay. They didn't even round up for that half-year.

Within two weeks Mark moved to California for a new job and I lost my earnest money on the condo.

He barely bothered to break up with me before he left. As in he barely said the words. Do you know how much it sucks when someone *insinuates* a break-up but doesn't actually do it? It's complete shit, is what it is. I basically had to break up with myself. Thanks, asshole. He said he was moving to San Francisco and I—stupidly, as it turned out—asked what that meant for us. He frowned at me and said something about it being a bit far, like I was dense for not getting it. "This is a really important time for me, Violet," he said.

Some girl named Lindy has him now.

So I really do need this.

As I approach the bus the doors slide open and the driver bounds down the steps with a huge grin. "Daisy!" he calls out, eyeing my tits.

Fuck. He knows me. I mean her. He knows my sister.

CHAPTER SIX

Violet

"Hey." I smile and glance at his name badge. George. Fuck, fuckity fuck it. Tom was supposed to be the driver this week. Tom Masey, who Daisy assured me she'd never met. Not George whoever this is, who she's obviously met. "George," I repeat and put a little enthusiasm into it. "Hey!" I wonder how many trips they've done together. How well does he know her mannerisms? This is going to be so much harder if he expects me to act like her.

He stops too close to me and flashes a smile, dimple flashing in his cheek. He's attractive and as he slides an arm around my waist in greeting it hits me loud and clear how well he knows Daisy.

I'm going to kill her.

"George," I say as I wiggle out of his embrace and try not to panic. "I thought Tom was my driver this week?"

"He was. When I saw you had this trip I switched with him." He winks. "He took my Boston to Maine tour."

"You can do that?" I question, then catch myself. "I mean, great." I nod and tighten my grip on my phone, still in my hand. I need to call Daisy. Then I need to grab my suitcase and run. No way can I do this. No way in hell. "You know, I just need to make a quick call," I say, pointing at the phone in my hand as I take a step backwards. But I don't even make it a second step before George has slung his arm around me again and rotated me to the bus door.

"Come on, Daisy, you can call from the bus. We've got to get on the road if we're going to make it to the airport in time to pick up the first group. You know staying on schedule is key."

"Um," I mumble, but he's on my heels so I find myself climbing the steps to the bus. It's a luxury travel coach, one I'm familiar with from the time I tagged along with Daisy. I climb the additional few steps past the driver's seat and face the empty bus before begrudgingly taking a seat in the first row. George snaps the doors closed and then buckles in, sliding a pair of sunglasses over his eyes as he maneuvers the bus out of the parking lot.

"So, Daisy," George starts as he stops at a traffic light on Frying Pan Road.

Do I stay or do I run? I mean, running is clearly the sane choice. But how do I get out of this now? Tell George I'm not Daisy? Tell George I'm suddenly ill and ask him to pull over? I could just start running, but a glance at the cars whizzing past the window tells me that running is probably not the safest idea.

But maybe she hasn't slept with him? Maybe they met once and he thinks he's got a shot with her. Daisy's a total flirt so that's possible. But I can't lean down and ask him how he knows my sister, can I? Since he thinks I am my sister. Jesus.

"Daisy?" George calls again but he doesn't get any further than that before I snap to attention and realize I've got less than ten minutes until we reach the airport. Less than ten minutes to figure out how to make this work, because I'm not a runner. I'm a pleaser. I'm a make-it-work kind of girl.

Also the thought of letting anyone down makes me want to throw up. I might like to strangle Daisy right now but I still don't want to let her down.

"I've got to make that call," I announce and stand up, gripping the handle on the seat edge for support. "It's private," I add as I take off down the narrow aisle to the back of the bus, already having hit redial with my thumb.

"Did you chicken out already?" Daisy asks as soon as the call connects. "It's been five minutes, Vi. Five minutes. This is not complicated. You stand by luggage carousel number one and hold up the Sutton Travel clipboard. The tour group passengers will find you. You check them off your list and send them out to the—"

"Daisy," I snap, cutting her off. "That's not why I'm calling. We have a problem."

"What's that, Violet?" she responds, but she doesn't sound worried. She never does. I've always sort of imagined that I came out of the womb with a skeptical frown while she followed a minute later with a high-five to the doctor. That we share the same DNA astounds me. Yet I can't imagine life without her.

"They didn't send Tom. They sent George," I tell her, my voice low. Not that I think George can hear me from this distance, but you can never be too cautious. "And George definitely knows you. He said he switched to get this route because of you."

"Huh," she replies after a moment of silence. "Well."

"Well?" I repeat, exasperated. "Elaborate, Daisy. I can see the airport from here. I don't have much time. How well do you know this guy?"

"I'm thinking. Which George is it?"

I take the phone away from my ear for a moment to stare at it in disbelief. "I'm guessing it's the George you know biblically, based on the way he was looking at me," I say, rolling my eyes and returning the phone to my ear.

"Right," she says, drawing the word out.

It takes me all of two seconds to work that out.

"You've slept with two bus drivers named George?" I hiss. "Who does that?"

"Probably a lot of girls," she replies, her tone unbothered. "The Georges are hot. And don't slut-shame me, Violet, you know it's ineffective."

"Obviously," I respond drily.

"Anyway," Daisy drawls, "which George is it? The hot one or the hot funny one?"

"How could I possibly know that, Daisy? I met him five minutes ago."

"Hmm, true. I guess it doesn't really matter which George it is. Just don't sleep with him. That would be weird."

"You think?" I reply sarcastically. We never ever date the same guys. We're close, but not that close. "What am I working with here, Daisy? Is either George in love with you? Do you have a pet name I'm gonna have to answer to? Will I have to break his heart?"

"No." She laughs and it comes out like a snort. "Neither George is in love with me," she says. "Definitely not," she adds and it sounds slightly sad.

"We're at the airport. I've got to go," I tell her. "You're my pea."

"You're my pod. Love you."

CHAPTER SEVEN

Violet

I'm exhausted. After the trip to the airport this morning I made sure the passengers got checked into the hotel and understood where to meet me this evening. Then I did the same thing all over again for the afternoon pickup. I tensed just a little every time someone asked me a question, worried I wouldn't have the answer. Add to that, I had George to avoid. Avoiding people is hard work. You've got to know where they are every second so you can make sure you're not in the same place at the same time. Or that if you are, you've got a lovely couple from Australia with you as a buffer so that the person you're avoiding can't offer you his room number. Just for example.

I'm gonna have to nip that in the bud.

I glance at the bed in my room and consider lying down for just a few minutes, but practicality wins out. I have an hour of free time before I need to meet the group downstairs. I look at my passenger list to triple-check I'm not missing anyone. We only picked up thirty-two from the airport today. The remaining nine made their own arrangements or came into town earlier, but the hotel tells me they've all checked in. So I can check that off my list.

Forty-one guests accounted for. Check.

I confirmed the hotel bar has a section set aside for our group tonight and will be serving a small buffet of finger foods promptly at six. Check.

I called the local guide we'll be meeting tomorrow and verified the location our group will meet her. Check.

Satisfied, I flip open my laptop and check my email to see if I've heard from any job prospects. Nothing, I note while biting my lip. I blow out a breath and send a couple of follow-up emails to recruiters I've been working with before taking a quick look at my preferred job websites. I manage to send a couple of résumés out before it's time to shut down and head downstairs. I step in front of the mirror and smooth my hands over my blouse. Daisy's blouse, technically. There's no uniform for the tour guides, thank God. The drivers have a uniform. Black pants, a dress shirt, a vest and depending on the weather a jacket on top of that. It's actually rather attractive, if you're into that sort of thing. Daisy's obviously into that sort of thing, I think with a smirk. Gotta love my sister.

Anyway, the guides don't have a uniform. They're not allowed to wear shorts or jeans. No t-shirts. Business casual, Daisy said as she packed her suitcase and handed it to me. "I lent you a few things. That sundress you always borrow without asking and the pink skirt I just bought are in there," she added while I stared at her like she was a lunatic. Obviously that exchange ended with me agreeing to this, so clearly I'm nuts as well.

For what must be the hundredth time, I cannot believe I agreed to do this. But it's time I got my groove back. Daisy's not wrong about that. And while impersonating my sister as a tour guide for Sutton Travel isn't my idea of getting my life together, it's a start. The pay isn't bad and I desperately need the infusion of cash. Plus the tourists traditionally tip the guide and driver at the end of the trip and Daisy promised that adds up to a nice little bit.

Besides, I really needed to get off her couch.

Daisy's got some great clothes, I muse as I twirl a bit in the pink skirt. I'm totally keeping a few of these outfits she packed for me. Bonus pay. She owes me that much for dumping this job on me, because her reasons are not entirely altruistic. If I know my twin, she's up to something this week.

So I'm going to make the best of this. That's kind of my motto anyway. Find a way to excel no matter what life throws at you. I'm done wallowing and I'm turning over a new leaf. The battery to my life needed a jumpstart and this is it.

That guy last night was one hell of a jumpstart, I think, grinning at myself like an idiot in the mirror. I can't help it, I'm feeling pretty smug about how brazen I was. I feel oddly... proud of myself. Is that normal? To be proud of a one-night stand? Well, I am.

Last night life threw a sexy British guy my way and I made the best of it—and I didn't even have a cheat sheet from Daisy to make it happen. Technically that article from the women's magazine might have given me a push, but I did it. I walked into the bar and smiled at him, didn't I? So yes, I'm a bit proud today.

I'm going to make this week my bitch. I've got my cheat sheet and my confidence back. I blow out a breath and straighten in front of the mirror. I've got a ton of résumés floating around. I sent a few more today and I've got two recruiters who believe in me and will call as soon as they have a job lead. They might even call me this week. You never know.

I grab the cheat sheet for the welcome dinner along with the complimentary Sutton Travel tote bags and lanyards for each passenger and head downstairs, a huge smile on my face. Things are definitely back on track and Daisy is right: No one is going to question it if I mess something up. They won't even notice.

Mr. Magic Mouth. Who knew one night with that man would provide such a needed boost to my self-esteem? Dare I look for him again tonight? Would he want a repeat? Or is he already onto his next conquest with a woman more permanent than myself? No, not going to think about that. I wanted a one-night stand and I got it.

CHAPTER EIGHT

Jennings

At six Nan and I stroll into the small dining area attached to the hotel bar. There's a sign indicating the area is reserved for our Sutton Travel group, so we find two seats at an open table and settle in. Three ladies traveling together from Canada join us shortly and Nan chats with them while I nod along and look at my watch, surveying the group I'm to spend the next week traveling with.

Retired couples mostly. This group of girlfriends on a girls' holiday at our table. A few couples in their thirties, perhaps. One or two who appear to be traveling alone.

It's interesting to watch a group of complete strangers from around the world forge an instant bond over a shared holiday. Bloody boring for me, but lovely for these people. The trip is off to a good start—people mingling and laughing, introducing themselves with a nod and a smile while exchanging notes about where they're from and commiserating on long flights and travel exhaustion.

And then the girl from last night walks in. Straight into the area cordoned off specifically for the travel group. So I tune everything else out and focus on her.

She's even lovelier than she was last night, if that's possible. That glorious black hair is pulled into a ponytail, the ends of it curling in thick waves. Her lips are painted a pale pink and her eyebrows are slightly raised in concentration as if she might be looking for someone. Is she looking for someone? Her eyes dart about the room as I mentally run through the group I was just observing and try to match her with any of them. Who could she be here with? Traveling with a friend perhaps? I've noted a handful of solo travelers in the group but she doesn't look like she belongs with any of them, nor did I observe any of them saving a seat.

She's wearing a white cotton blouse. It swells slightly over her breasts and I most definitely want another go with her. Knowing what she looks like underneath that blouse is torture. Perfect rosy tits on that one. The way they felt resting in my palms and the sounds she made when I took them into my mouth. I need another taste.

Her tongue darts out to wet her lips, then she sucks in a breath and opens her mouth to speak a millisecond before I realize she's gripping an armful of Sutton Travel tote bags and I suspect—if I was willing to take my eyes off of her to verify—the entire room has turned its attention towards her.

"Hello," she says to the group with a little wave of her hand. "Hello again, everyone, and welcome to the Highlights of History tour with Sutton Travel."

Bloody hell, she's the travel guide. I laugh out loud and her head turns towards me, the smile dropping straight off her face when her eyes land on mine. Her perfect bottom lip drops and her eyes flare before she does her best to recover, whipping her gaze away from mine with an, "Um," to the assembled group while tucking a nonexistent stray strand of hair behind her ear.

"So, um, welcome!" she repeats, but her voice is a bit breathless now and she's fidgeting. And her eyes are everywhere but on mine. She shifts her weight from hip to hip and I relax back in my chair and kick my legs out in front of me before folding my arms across my chest with a grin. This trip just got a hell of a lot more entertaining.

What the heck is her name then? I don't recall the guide for this trip being called Rose. I pull up the agenda on my mobile to confirm the itinerary and one Miss Daisy Hayden is the guide assigned to the Highlights of History tour this week. There's even a picture of her at the bottom of the email, a generic welcome the company sends. Perhaps I should have opened it before picking her up in the hotel bar last night, I muse while another smile crosses my face, but this is more fun. So she's a Daisy. I stare at her while contemplating that. I'm not sure it suits her; she reminds me of a rare flower, not a common one. Not that Rose was any better, but it's cute the way she stuck to a flower theme for her alias.

"I met most of you earlier today during the airport pickups," she starts with another glance darting in my direction, "but for the rest of you, my name is Daisy Hayden and I will be your guide this week on the Highlights of History tour." She speaks with a wide smile but she seems nervous. She was more confident last night picking me up in the bar than she is right now. She rattles on about the forecasted weather for tomorrow and the amount of walking we can expect during tomorrow's sights. Reminders about the importance of staying on schedule and notifying her if we plan to skip any of the scheduled activities so she knows not to look for you. Then she invites everyone to enjoy the buffet that's been set out for us.

She manages to do this without meeting my eyes one single time. I catch her darting glances in my direction, her gaze making its way around my table companions but never coming to a stop on mine. Meanwhile I can't take my eyes off of her. Beautiful. The way her ponytail sways as she places the stack of tote bags on an empty table, brushing against her arm as she bends slightly. How her brows draw together in concentration when a guest asks her something I can't make out from across the room. The curve of her calves and the delicate shape of her ankles, the sensible ballerina flats on her feet. I'm a goddamned arse for letting her get away this morning, but now I've got another chance. Fate, if you will. And judging by this group and the itinerary, she'll be done with her tour guide duties each evening with time to spare.

Time best spent with me. In bed.

Yes, I plan to become very well acquainted with Miss Hayden this week.

Once the group rises and heads towards the buffet queue the smile drops from her face and she finally sneaks a peek back at me. Her eyes widen when she finds me staring unabashedly back at her and then she spins, her soft pink skirt twirling with her as she exits the restaurant with her head down, thumbing something across the keypad of her phone.

I tell Nan I need to make a business call and encourage her to go ahead and eat with her new Canadian friends while I step out for a bit. Then I follow Miss Hayden and find her outside in the hallway as I'd expected, betting that she can't run off until the welcome dinner is over. She's half hidden behind a large decorative planter, one hand holding the phone to her ear and the other pressing against her opposite ear to block out the background noise.

"No, I told him my name was Rose," she hisses into the phone. Her back is to me and I stop just opposite the planter because why the hell not? Who am I to overlook a golden opportunity to gain a bit of information?

"Why? I don't know why, it just seemed like a good idea at the time. I thought we were doing a fake name thing. I've never had a one-night stand so I didn't know what the protocol was."

I smile at that and I'm glad she's not facing me because I know my smile is likely rather pompous, but I can't help the satisfaction I feel about being the one to take that honor.

There's a pause as she listens to whoever is on the other end.

"I'm not slut-shaming you, I'm explaining," she says with an exaggerated sigh. "And you're prude-shaming me when you laugh. It's very hypocritical, Da—" She turns as she speaks and stops mid-sentence when she sees me standing there. "I've got to go," she whispers into the phone and I smile. It's a bit late for whispering.

"You," she says in a tone that doesn't exactly imply that she's glad to see me. Her hand clenches into a fist then relaxes as she stands a little taller and shakes her head. She pulled the end of her ponytail over her shoulder during the call, wrapping a curly lock of it around her fingers as she talked. It rests against her blouse and I'm inclined to reach out and touch it but I don't think she'd allow that just now.

"Yes, me," I agree. "Still Jennings, by the way," I add with a smirk. She bristles in response. Her eyes flare before narrowing while her lips turn downwards and her arms cross against her chest defensively. "So it's Daisy then, not Rose," I say, testing the way it sounds on my tongue. "I wouldn't have guessed you for a Daisy."

"Well, I am," she retorts. "A Daisy," she states, just to be sure I'm clear. Then she frowns. "Why don't I seem like I could be a Daisy? Daisys have all the fun." She waves her arms wide to encompass all the fun she is capable of and I bite back a smile.

"Fair enough."

"Anyway, I thought you were here for business," she hisses. "Not on a vacation with your sugar momma."

"Grandmother," I correct. I am here on business, if indirectly. I should tell her that. I should.

"Fine." Her shoulders drop and she shrugs one shoulder. "Your grandmother. You're on vacation with your grandmother," she repeats, drawing the word out. "You're almost forty and your grandmother is still paying for your vacations. Way to go." She taps her fingers against her forehead and closes her eyes for a moment while shaking her head.

Come again? She thinks my nan is paying for this trip… oh, she's priceless. And I can work with that. "Dreadful, isn't it? The economy and all isn't what it used to be." I place my hands in my pockets and lean an inch in her direction before speaking again. "But let the journey begin, right?"

That's the tagline for Sutton Travel. *Let the Journey Begin.* I think it'll get me a smile but she just looks at me like I'm an idiot.

"Listen, Jennings." She takes a deep breath and shifts her eyes away from mine. "I'm sorry about last night."

She's sorry?

"I didn't realize you'd be on this tour," she continues in a rush. "I hope this won't be too awkward."

"Why would it be awkward?"

Her eyes fly back to mine with her brows raised in disbelief. They're the deepest blue framed by thick dark lashes. She's so very lovely.

"Um, because you've seen me naked?"

My lips slide into a lazy grin as I take in her earnest

expression and the slight blush on her cheeks. "Indeed, I have seen you naked, love," I agree while running my gaze slowly over her head to toe and back again. "Nothing awkward about that at all," I add as she fidgets and the blush on her face surpasses slight. "But I thought you normally saw the men you slept with more than once, so seeing me again shouldn't be an issue for you, should it?"

Her eyes flare as she realizes I most certainly heard that little tidbit about being her only one-night stand. I grin while she scowls.

"But not at work," she whispers. "And not without knowing their last names and stuff," she adds with a little shake of her head. "This is already a disaster," she says more to herself than for my benefit.

"Jennings Anderson," I offer while holding out my hand. "And I like steak, hate popcorn and love puppies. Now you know my name and some things about me." Some, but not all. Not the part she'd find most interesting.

She tilts her head and narrows her eyes before speaking. Dubious. That's what I'd call the look on her face. Dubious. "Yes, well, Jennings, if you'll excuse me I have a job to do." She nods at the room behind me where the tour guests are dining.

"By all means, love," I agree, moving aside and holding a hand up in the direction of the restaurant. "I'll let you get back to work then. Wouldn't dream of distracting you from your job," I add with a wink.

"You already are," she mumbles as she moves past.

If only she knew exactly how much I want to be her distraction. Every night. All week. *Yes, Miss Daisy Hayden, you have no idea how distracted you're about to be.*

CHAPTER NINE

Violet

Well, last night was a clusterfuck. That's my first thought when I wake up this morning. Cluster. Fuck. My alarm hasn't even sounded and I'm already awake and thinking about being stuck with my one-night stand for a week. Seven nights and eight days to be specific. Yay me.

How does this happen? I mean really, why does this stuff happen to me? I set out to have a slutty one-nighter and I end up with a guy I'm stuck with for a week. And I'll probably sleep with him again, so there goes my only one-night stand. Assuming he wants to sleep with me again, but I think he does. He seemed to enjoy himself last night and if I'm being honest, there's not a whole lot of competition this week. Most of the women on this trip are married or over sixty. Plus he looked amused as hell when he followed me into the hallway last night, during the welcome dinner. Of course he could pick up someone not on this trip in the evenings. Like he picked me up last night. Or did I pick him up? No, all I did was smile at him for three seconds. He sent the drink and joined me, so I guess there's that. But anyway, I think he's probably interested in a repeat.

So if I sleep with him again can I still count this? When I'm fifty and having drinks with girlfriends and reminiscing about our misspent youths, would it be cheating to say, 'Oh, yes, I had a one-night stand once. With a hot British guy. I even gave him a fake name. The entire thing was quite provocative?'

Good Lord, I'm an idiot. Like I'd use the word 'provocative' in casual conversation. And I only gave a fake name because I was impersonating my sister and I didn't want to give him her name, because that would be weird.

Oh, fuck.

Fuckity fuck!

I sit straight up in bed and stare at the blank television across from the bed. I can't sleep with him again now that he thinks my name is Daisy. I mean, what if he calls me Daisy while we're having sex? Nope. Just no way.

I think I'm gonna cry. I'm trapped on a week-long tour with Magic Mouth and I can't even enjoy it. Why does the universe hate me? Why? I flop back onto the bed with a loud and annoyed groan before snatching my cell off the bedside table to check the time. Looks like I might as well get up. My alarm is set for half an hour from now and I'm sure as heck not going to fall back asleep now.

My mind is racing. Racing with terror at faking my way at playing tour guide this week. And racing with memories of what it felt like to sleep with Jennings. I'm turned on just remembering it. The way he felt on top of me, inside of me. The way it felt to be stretched around his cock. His lips—shit, I shiver remembering his lips. And he was good with them. Everywhere. On my neck and trailing down the inside of my arm, the spot behind my ear and above my bellybutton. And lower too. Oh, good Lord, did he know what he was doing.

Well, forget him. The sex probably wouldn't be as good the second time anyway. It'd probably be average if we did it again, totally average. The first time was probably toe-curling perfection because it was a little forbidden: sex with a hot stranger I was never going to see again. Sex without any of the anxiety about if I was making it good for him or caring if my body made any weird sex noises in the midst of all that thrusting, because holy shit, I was drenched for him. Like embarrassingly wet. Kinda like I am right this moment thinking about it.

It was probably just that hot because it was new dick. Yup, that's it. That's the reason: new perfectly-sized dick. Thick enough to feel it and long enough to wince when he slid in all the way in with his pelvis resting on mine. Attached to an impressively nice body with a face that makes me want to drop to my knees and take him in my mouth. And the British accent didn't suck. Sweet baby Jesus, the accent. I'm screwed.

I kick the covers off and head for the shower with another groan. Looks like a cold shower is in order to head off a long and sexually frustrating day.

Ninety minutes later I'm downstairs in the hotel restaurant. The trip includes breakfast each morning at whichever hotel we're at that day, so I see most of the group wandering in or out and enjoying the buffet set out by the hotel. I nab a banana and a cup of coffee then sit at an empty table with today's agenda. I just have to get everyone onto the bus, count them twice to make sure I'm not missing anyone and then recite some tidbits Daisy jotted down for me about Washington while we make the drive into the city. Once we get downtown we meet up with the local specialist who will take us on a walking tour around the National Mall. All I have to do is trail behind the group and then when that's over I give them a couple of hours to explore on their own and a location for everyone to meet back up. Easy enough.

The chair across from me slides out and I glance up to find George taking a seat. Shit, why did I sit at a table alone? I managed to avoid him all day yesterday but my time just ran out. He's here, and I'm cornered, so to speak.

"Daisy," he says with a seductive grin. "I thought I'd see you last night." He raises an eyebrow in question and I have to admit he's very attractive. He's Daisy's type for sure—dark hair, blue eyes and a big ego. And then I remember he thinks I'm Daisy and that he gave me his room number yesterday. I kinda forgot about that when my one-night stand problem smacked me in the face.

"Um, George," I start but he slides his hand over mine on the table and catches me off guard. I move my eyes from his to our hands and back again when a throat clears to my right and I snatch my hand back as I glance over.

It's Jennings.

Of course it's Jennings.

He's in jeans and a polo shirt and manages to look like he stepped out of a Brooks Brothers ad, or whatever the British equivalent is.

I flush just looking at him, but I'm not sure he's similarly affected. If I had to guess I'd say he was annoyed, not aroused.

"Good morning, Miss Hayden." He nods in my direction before turning his attention to George. "George." He nods to George, his tone dismissive. After a long pause where Jennings makes no move to leave, George glances between us, then announces he's going to prep the bus and takes off.

Well, that's one awkward exchange with George avoided.

Cue awkward exchange with Jennings instead.

"Where's your grandmother?" I ask as Jennings takes the seat George just vacated and hope in vain that he isn't interested in reminding me about his amazing sex skills. I suppose that's an overly specific worry and probably not likely in the midst of a free breakfast buffet, but yeah, that's exactly where my mind goes.

"Are you involved with the driver?" He ignores my question and asks his own, his eyes narrowed on mine, his jaw tight. Annoyance confirmed.

"What? No!" I scoff, then bite my lip. Well, I'm not, but Daisy is. Or she was. Shit, this is sort of complicated. "Not really, no."

"Not really?" He raises a brow and leans closer to me over the table. "You're not certain?"

"I mean, no?" I respond and I know it comes out more like a question than an answer. "*I'm* not," I add, pointing to myself with my hand with a little shake of my head. But then I scrunch my nose a little and look away, which probably makes me seem guilty, as if I am involved with George.

"I don't share," he states when I meet his eyes again.

He says it in that posh British accent. 'I don't share.' And yeah, I'm thinking about him naked all over again and my breath catches in my throat because who says, 'I don't share?' He might as well have growled, 'Mine,' and to be honest I never thought I'd experience a man pulling such an alpha stunt in my lifetime.

It doesn't suck.

I grin.

He scowls.

I laugh.

He doesn't.

"I'm waiting, Miss Hayden," he states and I swear his jaw ticks. I've never known a man who could actually do that before either. It also doesn't suck. I don't want to goad him but the jaw ticking thing is quite enjoyable and I wouldn't mind seeing it again.

"You're upset at the idea that I could be involved with George?" I question unnecessarily and try not to grin again, his mood not indicating he's interested in joking. "No, I personally am not involved with George. Does that make you happy?"

"It does, Daisy." He nods and the lines around his eyes relax as he sits back a bit in his chair.

Daisy. Ugh. Hearing Daisy's name coming from his perfect lips feels like being offered a glass of cold tap water after shoveling a foot of snow off the sidewalk when you were hoping for a mug of hot chocolate with some marshmallows floating on top. Time to rip the Band-Aid off.

"This has nothing to do with George, but I can't sleep with you again, Jennings," I say in a rush while he stares at me, his head tilted to the side and his hand running along his jaw. His expression is impassive, his eyes contemplative. Oh, fuck. Maybe I got this wrong? Maybe he has no interest in a repeat performance with me? I feel like an idiot and my cheeks heat up in embarrassment. "Assuming you wanted to, that is. Assuming you wanted to do it again." I pause. Do it again? I sound like a teenager and I have to make a concentrated effort not to slap my forehead with the palm of my hand. Total idiot. "Did you want to though?" Why am I still talking? "Never mind, the answer is no."

Wait, he said he didn't share, which meant he thought we would sleep together again. Right? Or did he just mean it in like a general way? Like, 'Hey, I'm not into being your side piece?' Do people still say that? Side piece? Or does he think I'm a cheater? Like, 'You should have told me you were already sleeping with some guy named George before you let me make you come harder than you ever have in your life?' Or maybe he meant it in a 'I don't do group sex' kind of way. Like, 'Hey, I'm not going to tag-team you with George.'

"I can't," I repeat with a small shake of my head. "Nope," I add awkwardly, popping my lips around the word. I need to shut the hell up. I stop talking and grab the banana resting on the table in front of me and peel it to keep myself busy, glancing anywhere but at him as I do so. Ah, there's his grandmother, sitting a few tables over with the Canadian trio. They appear to be old friends already, chatting away and laughing over something or other. I shove the banana into my mouth and wonder if Jennings is going to respond to my little outburst or just keep staring at me. I dart a glance back in his direction. He drops his eyes from mine, runs them slowly down the banana between my lips and then back up to meet my eyes again. And then I choke.

I drop the banana and cough into my hand.

Now he smiles, the dirty bastard.

"Why?"

"I have to have a reason?" I snap in return because now I'm annoyed.

"Fair point," he agrees with a nod. "No, you don't."

"That's right, I don't." It comes out a little smug but I'm sort of relieved that I wasn't wrong about his interest. "I met you two days ago. I don't have to give you a reason why I'm not interested in sleeping with you again."

"Two days ago when you propositioned me in the hotel bar."

Err, I should probably take the smug level down a notch.

"Two days ago when you told me"—he pauses here while I wonder what idiot thing came out of my mouth that he's about to repeat—"that you were a sure thing."

Right. That. I blow out a breath and stare at him while I think. I must be doing a shit job of hiding the fact that I'm thinking of something to say because he has a really amused smirk on his face.

"Maybe I have a kink where I only have sex with strangers."

"We both know that's not true," he says easily and motions with his fingers for me to continue with my next objection.

"Maybe I didn't enjoy it that much," I offer.

"Try again, love."

Yeah, he's right, we both know I enjoyed it. I wonder how flushed I am right now at the mere memory.

"It's just that it's against company policy," I say. I have no idea if that's true or not but it's got to be true, right? Sleeping with customers cannot possibly be allowed.

"Is it?" he questions, his brows up, seemingly genuinely interested in this.

"Yeah." I nod and try to look confident. I add a little shrug when he doesn't immediately respond.

"Well, isn't Sutton Travel lucky to have such a dedicated employee," he muses after a moment.

"Yeah," I say again, but this time it comes out a little doubtful. Daisy's a terrible employee! She sent me on this trip in her place and I have no idea what I'm doing! And she doesn't even care if I get fired or not. Or she gets fired, whichever.

"I'd hate for you to cock up your job," he says and I wonder if 'cock up' is a British phrase or if he's talking dirty to me.

"Yeah," I say for the third time and this time I'm sad. Freaking twin problems. And lies. They're so complicated.

"Of course, we knew each other before I was a customer, didn't we? A pre-existing relationship, if you will. That can't possibly count." Wait. He really does want me again? This gorgeous, sexually talented man wants *me* again.

"Well," I start. "I don't—"

"That's sorted then," he says and pushes his chair back. "I'll see you on the bus, Miss Hayden."

CHAPTER TEN

Jennings

I still think she's lying about something, but as long as she's not fucking the driver I suppose it doesn't matter. Except I hate being lied to. Bloody hate it, which is hypocritical as hell since I'm lying to her as well.

I wasn't at first. I didn't say a single untrue thing when I met her. But I'm lying to her now, aren't I? By omission, I suppose, but still a lie. A smallish one. Nearly insignificant. To me anyway. To her it might be another matter entirely.

She's different, this girl. I smile thinking of her fumbling through her list of excuses to avoid seeing me again. Please. She came three times. Loudly. So if she's not seeing the driver then what is it? It can't be some moral quandary about sex, can it? We've already done the deed so what would another few tumbles matter? She was quite keen when she thought I was a stranger—and that hasn't changed, not really. She can't be such a rule-follower she's worried about some supposed Sutton Travel company policy—if it even exists.

I wonder what she does when she's not guiding tours. Where she lives, if she's got a flatmate or perhaps a cat.

How far she could take me down her throat.

Just everyday thoughts, really.

"Jennings, darling, thank you for taking me on this

trip." Nan interrupts my musings as we exit the hotel and walk the short distance to the coach parked just out front. "I know how busy you are but I do so look forward to my annual trip," she says with a pat to my arm. "Besides, it's all quite informative, isn't it?"

"Very informative, Nan," I agree.

I'm only here to appease Nan. When the trip ends I'll deliver her to my aunt Poppy in Connecticut for the remainder of the summer. Then I'll be on the first flight to London.

"Very good, and I've always wanted to take this tour. Time well spent for both of us then."

I nod my head in agreement as we board the bus. Her new Canadian friends immediately wave us over to some empty seats near them as the coach doors close and Daisy walks down the aisle taking a head count, her lips moving as she counts to herself, her eyes rolling as they pass mine. Not too worried about policy then, is she? I'd think eye-rolling customers must be prohibited, but Lord knows with the Americans. She returns to the front of the coach, signaling to George we're good to go, and then turns on the microphone system with an enthusiastic, "Good morning," to the group.

"So, um, welcome again to Sutton Travel Highlights of History tour. Glad you all made it on time this morning, thank you for that." She smiles brightly but her hand is gripping the microphone so hard her knuckles are white. As if she's responsible for passing the baton during an Olympic relay sprint instead of delivering a few dull tidbits to a group of tourists. She clears her throat before continuing, reminding us what's on the agenda before picking up a small notepad and glancing it over. Does she really need notes in order to do this?

She nods to herself then tucks the notebook away

before asking the group to pull the tiny radio-controlled boxes from the seat pockets in front of each seat. After handing each guest a set of cheap disposable earbuds, she runs the group through testing the headset. The boxes operate on a simple on/off switch and volume dial so that lesson goes quickly. We'll use them as we walk and the local guide narrates via the headsets.

Once that's all sorted Daisy's shoulders relax as she turns on a promotional video on the overhead monitors and drops into the empty row of seats directly above and behind the driver. I'm five rows behind her so I can't hear her sigh, but I imagine she does. Is she nervous about this tour or about me? Neither makes much sense. Both intrigue me.

"Jennings, would you mind if I sat in the empty seat next to Vilma?" Nan breaks into my thoughts and gestures to her new friends. "It'll be easier for us to chat."

"Not at all. I think I'll go up and join the guide. I've got a few questions for her."

"Oh, great idea, you do that!" Nan readily agrees, patting my knee just as she did when I was a boy. "I'm so thrilled you've taken such an interest in the tour."

So am I. But I don't think it's in the way she's thinking.

Daisy's in the window seat, so she doesn't have a chance to object when I slide into the empty aisle seat next to her. Her head snaps up from a notebook clutched in her hand, her expression turning into a scowl when she sees me.

"You can't sit there," she says.

"I think that I can," I respond, unbothered by her sass. I slide my arm over the headrest behind her and lean into her ear. "Are you this rude to all the tour guests or just the ones you've slept with?"

Her mouth drops open and her eyes widen in shock before she recovers.

"Just you," she states, narrowing her eyes at me before returning her attention to the notebook in her hand. She quickly snaps it shut and holds it on her lap, her fingers curled around the edge.

"What have you got there?" I nod to the notebook. In my mind it's a journal, filled with dirty thoughts about me.

"Nothing. Just notes about the trip," she says with a shrug.

"Ah." I nod. The dirty notes were a long shot but still, I'm disappointed. "How long have you been a tour guide, Daisy?"

"Uh, a few years," she says, but she won't look at me.

"A few?"

"Yeah, a few. How about you? How long have you been mooching vacations off of your grandmother?"

"Mooching? What a brilliant word. I assume it's an American term for getting a handout?"

"It is," she confirms, unabashed.

I grin. "Well, I have been the apple of Nan's eye since the day I was born."

"Yeah, okay," she agrees in a tone riddled with sarcasm.

"So what do you need the notes for? If you've been doing this a few years it should be old hat by now, shouldn't it?"

"It's a new tour," she responds.

"Is it?"

She glances at me before quickly looking out the window. "Newish," she replies with a shrug. "For me," she adds.

She's evasive about the oddest things, which only

serves to intrigue me more.

When we reach the outskirts of the National Mall the bus stops and the group disembarks while Daisy confers with the local guide. George stays with the coach, which suits me fine. I still don't like him.

Daisy does yet another head count, then ensures everyone has their headset on and can hear. The guide takes off while delivering her spiel on the history of the Washington Monument. I watch the guests follow along for a few minutes while Daisy lags at the rear of the group, making sure she doesn't lose anyone. Nan's group has positioned themselves near the front, keeping a careful eye on the local guide, headset boxes clutched in hands. There's a couple from Scotland with professional-looking camera equipment snapping pictures every few feet while the majority of the group just use their mobile phones.

I pull the earbuds off and shove them into my pocket along with the radio box.

"What are you doing?" She stops walking and looks at me suspiciously.

"I'm more interested in observing you than the tour," I tell her with a wink.

She groans.

I smile.

"Do you have a job, Jennings?" She squares her shoulders and looks at me as if she'll be able to assess the truthfulness of my answer.

"I do." I nod.

"Do you live with your mother?"

"I do not." I shake my head once and bite back a smile.

"Okay," she says, then pauses. "Do you live with your grandmother?" she asks slowly, her brow arched in suspicion as if I've found a loophole to avoid an honest answer.

"I do not live with my nan," I confirm.

"Okay," she finally says with a nod.

"Okay," I agree though I'm not sure what conclusion she's just drawn.

"We can have sex this week," she announces. "Because you're good at it," she adds and starts walking again. "And because that accent of yours drives me wild and because frankly, I don't need another reason."

"Well then, glad that's settled." I don't fight the smile this time. I can't recall a woman ever telling me I was good in bed in quite such an... ineloquent way before, but it's distinctly Daisy.

"Don't make me regret this, Jennings. You seem like trouble and I've got a lot going on."

"I'll make you come with as little trouble as possible," I promise.

"And for the record, I'm still going to count this as a one-night stand. Unless I have another one-night stand in the future, then I'll use that one, but if I don't then this one still counts."

"Right." I nod slowly even though fuck knows what that means.

"Okay then. We've got a deal."

"A sex deal?" I ask, wide smile on my face. "How kinky."

"You said you weren't going to be trouble," she says drily with a tilt of her head and a lift of her brow in challenge.

"Fair enough, that I did."

"Go join your grandmother, Jennings. I'll deal with you later."

Oh, I should hope so. I shake my head with another

grin, wondering what just happened. I don't normally have women so reluctant to give me attention. Or speaking to me like I'm a lost dog. Yet I'm smiling and curious about what she's going to throw at me next.

CHAPTER ELEVEN

Jennings

There was a group dinner tonight—included with the tour package. Billed as a premier dining experience or some nonsense. It was an agonizing affair that took up the better part of three hours. George was there, which I'm sure is customary but nonetheless annoying. He sat at a table with Daisy while I was across the room with Nan and a couple from Japan. Daisy spent the dinner looking anywhere but at George, which was somewhat mollifying. George for his part just looked confused.

The restaurant was medieval-themed, complete with dim lighting and food served on wooden platters set in the middle of the table and drinks served in pewter tankards. It was awful. Nan, however, was delighted by the atmosphere and everyone else appeared to be having a good time as well so clearly the issues were mine. I'd have taken a godforsaken American chain restaurant with utensils wrapped in a paper napkin over eating with my fingers, but all that matters now is that it's over. Thank fuck.

I spent most of the dinner forcing myself not to think about what Daisy looks like naked lest I get a hard-on. A mission accomplished, just barely.

But now we're back at the hotel for the night. Finally, blissfully back at the hotel. Tomorrow the tour moves to

Williamsburg, Virginia for two nights. But tonight, Daisy's tour guide work is just about done and I'll finally have her to myself.

I escort Nan to the lift and bid her a good night before retreating to the lobby to wait for Daisy. Circumspectly, of course. She's busy answering questions for a couple from the tour so I pretend to be interested in a rack of promotional flyers located in the lobby. I pick one up for a duck tour—an amphibious vehicle that drives the streets of DC before splashing into the Potomac River and cruising the rest of the tour. I give thanks that I won't be subjected to a ride on a hybrid car/boat and stuff the flyer back into the stand while watching Daisy nod along to whatever the couple she's speaking with is droning on about.

Watching her makes me think of my first job out of university. It's been... what, fourteen or fifteen years now? Fuck, was I ever twenty-two? For a moment maybe, a lifetime ago. My dad's voice rings loudly in my head, asking me if I have any intention of slowing down. I wonder if he doesn't have a point when I realize how fast the years are passing.

But they're passing so damn enjoyably, I muse with a glance at the lovely Daisy. I catch myself smiling and I have to physically swipe a hand over my mouth to wipe it away. Why slow down when I'm having so much fun?

Besides, work keeps me busy.

My passion has always been success. At work and with women. Right now one very specific woman. I watch her talk to another guest from the tour and wonder if I can skip past offering to buy her a drink tonight. I know it makes me some kind of barbarian arsehole, but I don't want to offer her a drink. I've been waiting for two days, I want her upstairs and naked.

Finally the last of the tour guests head towards the lifts and I note Daisy on their heels, as if I'm not standing here waiting for her. As if she's just going to slip upstairs without a word. I don't think so.

"Miss Hayden." I lay a hand lightly on her arm to stop her from proceeding and she huffs a bit, a cross between a sigh and an exhale as she flicks her eyes to mine. "I believe we have plans," I remind her.

"I've changed my mind," she says with a tiny insolent shrug.

Changed her mind? Bloody hell. She can't be serious. I look into her eyes, trying to gauge the situation, searching for a hint of mischievousness, but it's not there. She's serious? Why are women so irritatingly complicated? Was I not just musing about how much I enjoy them and now this? Vexing is what they are. Each and every last one of them is a different sort of exasperating, with their own unique combination of things that piss them off. A man's got to be a mind-reader to decipher what they're on about half the time, for fuck's sake.

I stare at her for a heartbeat, thinking it would make my life easier if I abandoned this straight away and found a different woman to spend tonight with, but dammit if she doesn't intrigue me.

"Whyever would you do that?" I find myself asking her instead.

"You're a customer," she replies, but her eyes fall to my chest and she swallows. A hint of a blush reaches her cheeks before she meets my eyes again. "It's not proper."

"Proper?" I can't help it, I laugh. "Are you living in Regency London now?"

"People still use the word 'proper,'" she scoffs at me. Literally scoffs. I'm not used to women being so transparent with me. She doesn't give a single toss about impressing me and it's sort of endearing in an odd way.

"Sure they do, as in 'I'd like a proper cup of tea.' No one uses the word to describe a sexual liaison."

"No one uses the word 'liaison' either."

"I think they do. Should we continue this conversation in my room?" I nod towards the lifts in hopes we're about done with this chat.

"No, Jennings. I'm serious." She stomps her foot a little when she says 'serious' and I'm not sure how I'll keep myself from kissing her right then, lobby be damned.

"What happened to you being a sure thing?" I question instead. "I quite liked you when you were a sure thing. Not that this little song and dance isn't fun."

"That was before."

"Before what exactly?"

"Before I realized how complicated this is," she huffs, but she's not looking at me and doesn't seem that invested in her defense. I can't help but feel like there's something I'm not getting.

"What's complicated about this?" I run my fingertip along the bare skin between her elbow and wrist and she inhales quickly. "And what happened to the part where my accent drives you wild?"

"It does," she agrees. She says it entirely too primly for a girl capable of multiple orgasms, one whose nipples hardened from me no more than skimming her arm.

Besides, I don't care about her perceived rules.

"Plus, you're my one-night stand and if I sleep with you again then you're not technically a one-night stand."

Come again?

"Not technically a one-night stand," I repeat back to her.

"Right." She nods and her brow is furrowed over this.

"And it was perfect," she says on a big exhale of breath and waves her hand while I smile, because yes, yes, it was. "Really, really great," she continues. "So if we do it again my perfect one-night stand is shot and what if the next time I have a one-night stand it's bad? Then my only one-night stand is terrible and then I'd have to keep having them until I had another good one and—"

"Okay, stop talking." I hold up a hand, hoping it's enough to make her stop. I don't even know where to begin with what just came out of her mouth, but since I don't care to zero in on the idea of her with other men, I'll start with the obvious. "You enjoyed yourself the other night?"

"Yeah." She looks at me as if I'm an idiot.

"So much so that you don't want to do it again?"

"It's complicated, Jennings." She frowns. "This tour"—she pauses—"it's just complicated."

"What if it's better the next time?" I say, ignoring her tour nonsense.

"Not possible." She shakes her head.

"What if it's just as good as the last time?" I say, gritting my teeth. "What if we could have sex just as good as the first night every night for the next week?"

"I don't think so," she replies, but she says it with a hint of longing in her voice and a lingering glance at my lips.

"Enough of this. I'm not done with you." I say it firmly, perhaps a bit more so than I meant, but her eyes snap to attention with interest at my tone.

"Not done with me?" she questions and her tongue darts out to wet her bottom lip. No, I'm most definitely not done with her.

"No, Daisy, I'm not. I need you again." Her eyes widen and I know I have her interest. "I need to taste your sweet pussy again. I need to suck on those gorgeous nipples until you're begging for my cock." Desire fills her eyes and her breathing hitches. She wants this. I'm not done. "I need you to come until you've had more orgasms than you knew were possible and you're limp from exhaustion. I need you to ride me until your thighs shake and then I'll flip you over and taste your pussy all over again. Until you're sated beyond measure. So no, Daisy, I'm not done."

"Don't call me that," she blurts out.

"Don't call you by your name?" This is a new one for me. Her eyes widen as I stare at her. I thought I'd uncovered every bit of crazy a woman could throw at me by now, but this is new.

"It's just that I really liked it when you called me 'love,'" she says. She's flushed and speaking faster than normal, the crazy flying out of her mouth at record speed. "It's so British the way you did that, and the truth is I'm a bit of an Anglophile. My secret is out!" she adds with an odd little wink. "Let's go to your room. Just call me 'love,' okay?" She spins in the direction of the lifts, not waiting to see if I'm following.

Crazy or not, I'm following.

CHAPTER TWELVE
Violet

That was close.

Way too close. *Don't call me Daisy.* What an idiotic thing to say, but I'm not cut out for this kind of subterfuge. I blow a stray hair off my forehead and jab at the elevator call button a bit more forcefully than necessary while I mull over my predicament.

The thing is I do want to sleep with Jennings again—of course I want to. I'd have to be insane not to want a repeat performance. I spent all afternoon daydreaming about it, recalling the details from the first time over and over again. The scent of his skin and the way it felt moving against my own. The way his hair stood up in spots where I tugged on it with my fingers. His magic mouth and brilliant fingers. The tilt of his head when he thrust into me and the look in his eyes as he came.

So yeah, sign me up.

Then by the time we got to dinner I started to think. What if he called me Daisy right in the midst of things? I don't think my psyche could ever recover from that blow. No way. He could have called me Rose—that would have been fine, a little naughty even, hearing him use a fake name I'd given him in the hotel bar. But my sister's name? No. Absolutely firm, great big huge no. So I resolved to stay away—better safe than sorry and all that.

But then he waited for me in the lobby. Pretending to look at tourism flyers while I pretended not to notice he was waiting. And then he was all convincing and suave and used words like... well, just words. He shouldn't be allowed to use words. Any of them. If he'd just grunted and given me his room key I'd have been able to resist. Probably.

But no, he used his sophisticated British accent to speak words and I'm not made of stone for crying out loud. He said 'pussy.' In the hotel lobby. In his accent and it was lewd and inappropriate and hot as hell. And then 'cock' flew out of his mouth and words like 'begging' and 'multiple orgasms' and, well, that was that.

So I blurted out the part about not calling me Daisy and nearly cost my sister her job a mere one day into this trip. I am literally the worst at undercover operations. It's pathetic. At twenty-six years old I should be better at deceit. I've got no game.

I wonder if I should just tell him? I bite my lip and glance at him over my shoulder. He's staring at my ass. I turn back around and look at the elevator button and wonder where the hell the elevator is. It's a three-story building, how long could it take to get back to the first floor? And why are we not taking the stairs? No, I can't tell him, I decide. What the heck would I say? *Hey, listen, the thing is I'm not actually Daisy. I'm Violet. Daisy's identical twin sister? Yeah, so she had something to do this week and I took her place as tour guide.*

I can't envision any scenario where that ends well. Or with me not in jail. *What's that, Jennings? No, no, I'm not a scam artist. Not technically. I was simply trying to earn some money from a job I'm not qualified for.*

Not a scam.

Right.

Holy shit, why didn't I think of this before now? I cannot have an arrest record or I am never getting another job again. This must be illegal, what we're doing. I'm so screwed.

When we finally step onto the elevator the mood feels somber. At least to me. Jennings might still be thinking about my ass for all I know, but he's quiet and so am I.

He pauses when we reach his door and waits until I meet his eyes. "You're not married, are you, Daisy?" he asks, then corrects himself with a roll of his eyes. "Love? You're not married, are you, love?"

"No." I shake my head. "No one's asked."

A hint of a smile pulls at his lips and he shakes his head as the lock clicks and he pushes the door open.

"Well then, that was an incredibly honest answer."

"I'm usually a very honest person," I tell him, and yes, I hear exactly how that sounds after the words are already out of my mouth.

"So you're usually an honest person." He examines me with interest as he flips the keycard onto the dresser. It slides across the surface and comes to a stop when it hits the base of a lamp.

"I'm not married, Jennings. Not engaged, not anything. I just get off on you calling me 'love.' I've got a fetish for all things British, that's all there is to it." I'm such a liar. At least most of that was true. I do enjoy it when he calls me 'love.' It'd be even better if he called me Violet, but I'm working with the cards I've been dealt right now.

"So you'd have said yes to any idiot who asked then?" He's back to that.

"Why are you assuming I date idiots?" Rude asshole. It's true, but still rude. He raises a brow to challenge my denial and I glare at him for a moment before speaking

81

again. "I was merely answering your question, Jennings," I reply in a bit of a huff. "You asked if I was married and I was detailing how *not* married I am by explaining to you that no one's asked."

"Well, I'm glad no one's asked, love."

"Um, thanks?" I reply, throwing him a look. "I'm sure marriage is a big joke to you, playboy, but it means something to some of us."

"I hadn't meant to imply it doesn't mean anything to me." He frowns. "Only that I'm glad you're unattached and here with me." He closes the foot separating us and brushes my hair back as he runs his lips down the side of my neck. "Very glad," he murmurs into my ear.

"Yeah, me too," I agree a moment before he covers my mouth with his own and I forget what we were even talking about. Damn him and his magic mouth. My entire body is warm and relaxed and I'm melting into him, my fingers snaking under his shirt to his chest. I'm happy I decided another round with him was a good idea.

"Now." He breaks the kiss and taps my bottom lip with his finger. "I want these lips on my cock, love."

I pause for a moment, too drunk on his lips to realize what he's just said. Then I swipe my lips with my tongue and gather my hair over my shoulders. "Did you just order me to suck your dick?" Holy crap, why does that make me so hot? I'm torn between glaring at him out of principle and begging him to say it again. I'm leaning heavily towards the begging.

"I did." He's blatant in his reply.

I eye his shirt, some vintage-looking concert tee from a band I've never heard of, but the way it lies across his chest has been distracting me all day. I push the hem up his chest until he takes over and flings it over his head, then I place my palms on his skin and lean in. "Say it again," I murmur, because yeah, I liked hearing it.

He grins as he lifts my blouse over my head then stops to fondle my tits over my bra. "Knees, love. I want to feel your warm, wet mouth wrapped around me. I want to see how much of me you can take and then I'll dig my hands into your hair and urge you to take just a little bit more, slide just a little bit deeper, suck a little bit harder."

I've dropped to my knees before he's finished speaking and I'm working his belt free, keeping watch on him from under my lashes. I pop the button of his jeans and yank the material to his knees without moving my eyes from his. Then I lean forward and kiss his flat abdomen while working my hands into his briefs and around him, pushing the fabric down as I do. And then I lose all my game.

"Oh!" I blurt out in surprise, hand still wrapped around his cock. I release him and sit back on my heels and look up. "What do I do with it?"

"What do you do with it?" He's looking at me like I've just claimed I'm a virgin.

"I've only seen regular dick before," I say with a shrug. I can't believe this escaped my attention the other night, but in my defense I never really got a look at it.

"Regular dick," he repeats with his posh British accent and a smirk, brow raised.

"You know, like the fixed kind? Um, circumcised!" I finally find the correct word and bounce on my heels a little while glancing between him and his dick.

"You American girls." He laughs while sliding his palm over the length of his cock and back again. I'm not sure if I should be grateful I'm not the first girl to be confused, or pissed off that this has happened to him enough to be a thing.

"I assure you it works quite the same," he tells me

while he strokes himself and his cock hardens.

Okay then, hard it does look exactly the same. I feel weirdly proud of myself for adding this experience to my sexual bucket list as I wrap my hand around his cock. I bet Daisy's never seen an uncircumcised penis. I'm certain of it actually, because she'd have told me about it if she had. Every detail, with hand gestures and a funny name for the guy. So I win this one. Twin win! I think as I try not to laugh. We used to say that to each other when one of us beat the other at something. I totally twin-win this one and I'm feeling pretty darn smug about it. Until Jennings asks why I'm laughing. While holding his cock in my hand.

"I'm just proud of myself," I tell him.

"For sucking my cock?"

"I mean, I wouldn't have articulated it quite like that, but sorta."

"So how much can you take then? If you're so proud?"

"Whoa." I hold up my other hand. "Don't get too excited. I can't deep-throat or anything." I shrug. "But I think I'm fairly decent at this. Hold on, let me focus." I slide my emergency elastic band off my wrist and gather my hair back into a pony.

"Are you serious right now?"

"What? It gets in the way. That is how dedicated I am to giving you a great blow job," I add as I finish with my hair and wrap my hand around him again.

"Are you worried you're going to be made redundant?"

"Make me redundant," I purr. "Is that British dirty talk coming out of your mouth?"

"Not quite, no." He shakes his head and the skin around his eyes creases in amusement.

"I take pride in my work, Jennings. In all things." I look up at him from under my lashes as I stroke my hand up and down the length of him slowly, back and forth. He's thick and heavy in my hand and my mouth waters at the anticipation of wrapping my lips around him. "Anything else I should know about your special dick?" I ask a moment before dragging my tongue up the underside of his cock, my movements slow but sure.

"Fuck," he hisses while twisting my pony into his hand to maneuver me to his liking. "No, I think you've got it."

I wrap my lips around him and swirl my tongue over the tip while rotating my hand around the length I can't reach with my mouth. His groan tells me I'm doing okay. As I bob my head over him I mentally pat myself on the back for having a few magic mouth skills of my own before I stop thinking of anything but pleasing this man. He tugs my hair and angles my head to the side so he can better watch me suck him off. The look of lust in his eyes fuels me and I'm tempted to touch myself but I'm more interested in touching him. Besides, I'd rather let Mr. Magic Mouth take care of me when I'm done, and I know for certain he will. Multiple times. That's what he promised me in the lobby and I don't doubt he'll deliver.

CHAPTER THIRTEEN

Jennings

There's no such thing as a bad blow job—at least there's never been one in my life. Some are more memorable than others certainly, but a woman with a willing mouth can't fail. And this girl is enthusiastic. And likely prefers drinking through a straw. Sweet Jesus.

She squeezes the length of me that her mouth can't reach with her hand, her wrist rotating with dexterity and her eyes not leaving mine until she withdraws my cock from her mouth with an audible pop. She dips her head and drags her tongue up the length of me from base to tip and makes me feel like a teenager worried about blowing my load too soon.

This girl, she charms me with her combination of naïveté and enthusiasm. The way she blurted out her proposition the first night with false bravado but then rode me with her hair tumbling over her shoulders and her eyes simmering with lust. How she sat back on her heels tonight asking me what to do with my cock then gathered her hair up as if she was getting ready to go on a jog before diving in with the eagerness of a professional.

The way she scowls at me during the day then laughs during sex with no regard for trying to appear sexy. She is sexy, possibly the sexiest woman I've had the pleasure of being with. But she's not trying to be. She just is, her combination of cautiousness and bravery intoxicating.

As is her mouth. Intoxicatingly soft. Enticingly warm. Blissfully wet. I urge her lower with a slight tilt of the hand I have wrapped around her ponytail and she gags slightly but keeps going. Like I said, enthusiasm is everything. She eases back then squeezes the base of my cock tighter with her fingers and slides me deeper than I'd have thought she'd be able to.

My balls tighten and I yank her head back before I can come down her throat. Not that I don't want to, but a warning is appropriate.

"I want it," she says before I have a chance to do more than groan as her lips clear the head of my cock. Her tongue wets her lips the moment the words leave her mouth. Her hand is still wrapped around the base of me, her thumb making firm swipes on the underside of my cock as she leans forward with her eyes on mine. "Give it to me, Jennings."

Bloody fucking hell.

I cup her jaw and slide my cock across the velvety surface of her tongue, her lips sucking me in, and spill myself down her throat with a grunt. When I've stopped she pulls back and swallows quickly, squeezing her eyes shut for a moment as she does and wiping the back of her hand across her mouth.

That little sequence should not be sexy but dammit if it wasn't. Sexy as hell because she did it for me, nearly winced when she swallowed. Fucking hell, that was hot. The innocence of it. As if I'm corrupting her a tad.

Then just as quickly she blinks before nodding her head. "Good, right?" she says with the tiniest hint of a smug smile and now I'm the one laughing.

"Better than good, love." I pull her to her feet and run my fingertips across her shoulder blades, easing her bra straps down as I do. "You were brilliant."

"Brilliant!" she repeats in a mock British accent with a wide grin. "I've definitely never been called brilliant before," she says and I find the idea of her doing this with someone more off-putting than I care to admit. I unsnap her bra and toss it onto the dresser so I don't have to see her furrow her brow over it landing on the floor. Then I do the same with her skirt before pushing her to the bed so I can slide her knickers past her ankles. They go with the rest of her clothes on the dresser before I crawl over her onto the bed, nudging her thighs apart with my knee as I do. Time to convince her tonight was a good idea, and that tomorrow night will be an even better one.

She sighs and spreads her legs further apart as I suck one of her perfect tits into my mouth. I cup the other with my palm and rub my thumb across her nipple and marvel at every splendid inch of her body. When I pinch her nipple her responding moan is music to my ears. Her legs tighten and she arches herself against me. The way her dark hair spreads across the pillows is a visual I'll use to pleasure myself to in the future, no doubt. I love the weight of her tits in my hands, the warmth of her skin when I suck her between my lips. She smells like a sunny day—some blend of coconut and citrus and heaven.

"Are you going to do that thing again?" Her hands are in my hair, her fingertips massaging my scalp, and I'd like it very much if she never stopped touching me.

"Thing?" I switch tits with my tongue and slide a hand lower so I can caress the skin where her small waist gives way to the delicate curve of her hip. I'll need to fuck her from behind before we're through so I can place my hands on her hips while she's kneeling before me, using the leverage to move her on and off of my cock while she—

"With your tongue," she says, interrupting my fantasy.

"I'm doing a thing with my tongue right now," I tell her and nip at her with my teeth in example.

"The other thing," she ekes out as she arches against me again, her fingertips pressing firmer in direct response to my teeth.

"This thing?" I ask as I move my hand from her hip and slide two fingers directly through her center, parting her. She's soaking and I'm grinning.

"Yup," she says, the word popping from her lips in a gasp. "That thing."

"Did you enjoy that thing, love?" I almost slip and call her Daisy. Why the bloody hell doesn't she want me to call her Daisy? What woman doesn't want to be called by her name during sex? It's beyond peculiar and I shouldn't give a toss, yet I find that I do.

But later. I'll think about that later. Right now I'll call her anything she damn well asks if it keeps her in my bed and under my tongue. Enveloping my cock with her wet pussy and screaming my name with her sweet mouth. Unlike her, I love hearing my name as she comes, her voice breathy and strained and filled with pleasure. Her American-accented pronunciations of 'don't stop' and 'right there' not so different from what I'm used to, but so much sweeter-sounding coming from her.

"Yes." She nods, her hair brushing across the pillow. "I did enjoy it. You should do it again. It probably won't be as good as I remembered it, but it's worth a shot."

"Right then." I shake my head and place a kiss on the underside of her breast. "I probably just got lucky the first time, didn't I?"

"You might've," she agrees. "I'll keep my expectations tempered."

"Off I go then." I smirk as I reposition myself, kissing her navel on the way. "I'll give it my best go."

"Uh-huh," she murmurs as I spread her apart and cover her with my mouth. Pleasuring this woman is something I'm only too happy to do. Hell, just thinking about it had me fighting off a hard-on all day.

She squirms as I suck her clit between my lips and her fingers tug on my hair in response. Interpreting her every twitch and sigh and learning how to make her groan harder and arch higher is the sole focus of my life at the moment. Her taste, her scent. The touch of her fingers. The tilt of her pelvis when she's close to coming.

I could assemble an encyclopedia's worth of ways to make her scream and it'd be time well spent.

But I've only got a week so I'd best pay attention. I can collect a notebook's worth of ways in that time, surely.

I discover that she's a little bit ticklish when a giggle slips out as I'm kissing her inner thigh and positioning her leg over my shoulder.

I learn that she tastes even better tonight than she did two nights ago.

I determine that she's not used to anal play when she jumps from a fingertip coated in her wetness circling her there, but that she comes pretty spectacularly when she lets me slip the finger inside.

I worry that a week won't be enough and contemplate taking more meetings stateside this year. Should I? Would she want that? I don't even know which state she lives in. Am I getting way ahead of myself? She's hiding something from me and I don't like deceit. But the real problem is this: I'm curious if it'll matter. Will whatever she's hiding be enough to break this spell she has on me?

CHAPTER FOURTEEN

Violet

I take a second head count, verifying everyone is on board before giving George the okay to hit the road. The suitcases have been counted twice and loaded underneath the bus and I haven't lost any guests. This tour guide thing is easy-peasy. Besides feeling like someone is going to yell 'You're not Daisy!' at any given moment, easy.

I drop into my seat with a small sigh of relief and check my notebook. Today we're traveling a couple of hours from Washington, DC to Williamsburg, Virginia where we'll spend two nights. But first we'll stop in Mount Vernon, home of the first American president George Washington, for a tour of his estate and then it's on to some revolution museum somewhere—I really need to check my notes.

Which is going to be difficult because Jennings has just deposited himself into the seat beside me.

"I believe we've established that you cannot sit there," I remind him without looking up from my notebook.

"We established that as a tour guest I sit wherever I like."

"First of all, that's not true. You're supposed to be in a seat rotation along with everyone else in order for everyone to get the chance to sit up front and enjoy the scenic view."

"I'm not taking up anyone's spot though, am I? I'm just taking this empty seat beside you."

"I'm working," I remind him.

"I can see that. Well done, you."

I turn to look at him now so he won't miss me glaring at him. I need him to go away so I can focus on this tour. It's bad enough that I'm hyper-aware of him to begin with, my idiotic heart beating faster whenever I know he's nearby. I sure as heck don't need him sitting right next to me. "What about your nan, Jennings? Shouldn't you be sitting with her?"

He winks at me and tilts his head towards the back where she's sitting. "She's made fast friends with the three Canadian ladies traveling together. It's easier for them to talk if they sit together." He shrugs. "So I'm odd man out, it seems."

I blow out a loud breath and shake my head. "How convenient for you."

"It is, isn't it?" he agrees as he holds up a piece of candy wrapped in cellophane. "I'm supposed to give this to you. It's a maple candy from the Canadians."

Of course it is.

"Checking your notes again?" he inquires with a glance at my notebook.

I snatch the candy out of his hand and twist the wrapper open then pop the candy into my mouth. I don't want a maple candy but I'll take it to buy myself a minute. Hmm, it's pretty good actually.

This man is a distraction. And while I'm enjoying the distraction, I can't risk one. If I get Daisy fired this week she's not getting paid for this tour. If she's not getting paid then I'm not getting paid—and that's a problem. My savings have dwindled to almost nothing and I can't live on my sister's couch forever. Or go to jail. Do people go to jail for impersonating another person if they had that person's consent? I'm in way over my head. And I will never get a new job with an arrest record.

"So what am I to call you during the daytime?" Jennings asks, interrupting my thoughts. "Am I to call you 'love' or is that reserved for when we're alone?"

Oh, yeah. Forgot about that problem.

"You can call me Daisy," I say as breezily as possible. "The 'love' thing is just a sexual fetish."

"I thought it was an Anglophile fetish," he reminds me. He's really turning out to be a pain in the ass. Which reminds me about last night. He might have a bit of an ass fetish with his roving fingertip. I had *no* idea a finger *there* could make me orgasm like I did. No idea. None. Nada. I sorta want him to do it again.

"That's what I meant, guv'nor," I say in a stupid British accent. Holy hell, someone stop me. "It's my sexual Anglophile fetish," I add in my normal voice with a nod. I sound insane. I cannot believe this guy wants to have sex with me. Well, maybe he won't after this. That'd solve at least one of my problems right now, wouldn't it? I really like having sex with him though.

Why is nothing in my life simple?

The friends I graduated with are married and on their first kid—if not their second. I'm playing twin switcheroo with my sister, hooking up with a stranger and finagling ways for him not to call me by my sister's name while we're having sex. Because he thinks I'm her. Sort of. I suppose technically he thinks I'm me and he's just confused about my name. Right? No, that's not right either. He thinks I'm a tour guide, which I most definitely am not.

I've got issues.

"I like barbecue potato chips," I blurt out. Daisy hates

them, which has been great for keeping her out of my snack stash while I live on her sofa, because who wants to share their unemployment potato chips? So I've just shared something about myself with him. Something about Violet and not Daisy. Then I physically slap myself on the forehead, because potato chips? Really? It's as if I'm trying to guarantee he never sees me naked again.

"Are you all right?" Jennings looks at me, confusion creasing his brow. He's got really nice eyelashes, I note. Super thick and dark.

"Yeah." I nod and look out the window. "I'm just tired."

"I should imagine so," he replies and I don't need to turn to look at him to know there's a satisfied smirk on his face because I can hear it in his voice. I turn anyway because I'm a glutton for looking at his face. He's attractive, and comfortable in his skin. Perfect jaw, full lips. I like to examine the few tiny lines I can find—they add character that intrigues me. Then his pocket rings so I look at his crotch instead. He tucks left, as it turns out. And now I'm thinking about sex again.

He pulls the phone from his pocket and glances at the screen before hitting the ignore call button.

"How far are we from our first stop?" he asks as he taps out a text. I wonder if it was a woman. I bet she doesn't even eat potato chips. Probably nothing but grilled chicken and kale. Do they have kale in London? Then I wonder why I'm wondering. Of course they have kale—it's not like London is in another universe. They probably eat it with their fish and chips or something.

"How would I know?" I mutter.

"Because you're the tour guide, Daisy. That's how you'd know," he says slowly, looking me over. "Are you sure you're all right?"

"I'm fine!" I wipe my palms against the fabric of my skirt and try to remember what the notes said. "We should be there in less than twenty minutes," I announce. I think that's right. One stop was twenty minutes and the other was two hours, who can remember which order they were in? A real tour guide, likely.

Maybe she's one of those women who eat whatever they want and don't get fat. Whatever. I can eat whatever I want like… twice a year and not gain a thing. "Will twenty minutes be suitable for you?" I ask as he taps away on his phone.

"Suitable?" he repeats as he keeps typing without looking at me. "I should think it'll be fine."

I should think it'll be fine, I singsong in my head, annoyed. Until my own phone rings. It's resting face up on the small flip down tray in front of my seat—and it's Daisy, her name flashing across the screen in what feels like foot-tall letters. I slap my hand over the phone and send the call to voicemail as fast as I can. Why didn't it occur to me to change how I have listed her in my phone? I flick my eyes to Jennings to determine if he noticed that the person calling me was, well, me. So awkward.

He seems absorbed in tapping out an email on his own phone so I breathe a sigh of relief and open the contacts so I can change Daisy's name. I wonder if I should change it to Violet? I hit the backspace button to retype before deciding that it will only confuse me more if my phone display tells me I'm calling myself. Ugh, what a mess. This is most surely going to end in disaster, but if it doesn't, I say a silent pledge vowing to never, not ever, let Daisy talk me into one of her shenanigans again. No matter how unemployed I might be or how convincing she might be. I backspace again and type 'Sister' onto the screen before hitting done and tapping closed on contacts.

That's when my phone rings a second time. I recognize the number even though it's not programmed into my phone. It's a job recruiter I've been working with. Yes! But I can't answer it right now. Not on a bus with no privacy and background noise. Dammit. I stare at the screen longingly for a moment before sending the call to voicemail while saying a silent prayer she's got good news for me.

It's not like she's going to change her mind because I couldn't answer the call, right? That's ridiculous. I'll call her back in the next hour—just as soon as we get to Mount Vernon. We've got a walking tour of George Washington's estate scheduled and I think once the tour starts I can fall behind the group and return the recruiter's call, along with Daisy's. I probably don't even need to follow the group through the walking tour, do I? When I tagged along with Daisy that one time she gave them free time to take pictures, visit the gift shop and all that jazz before they boarded the bus again. So I'll just deliver the group to the beginning of the walking tour and give them a spot to meet me at after and that'll free up a couple of hours for me to return calls and check my email. Perfect.

"Are you avoiding someone, love?"

It appears I have Jennings' attention again, his eyes on the phone I'm holding and nervously tapping my fingers against.

"No," I reply coolly. "Are you?" I question with a nod to his phone.

"Not at all." He laughs.

"Okay," I retort for lack of having anything else to say. Then I thump my head against the headrest and groan.

"Everything all right?"

"I've just got a lot going on." I shrug.

"Tell me about it," he says and he seems genuinely interested and I wish I'd met him as Violet.

"Do you ever wish you could start over?" I ask.

"You're pretty young to be worried about starting over, aren't you?" He says it quietly, then frowns while examining my face. "You've got your whole life ahead of you."

"I'm almost thirty." I sigh.

"You're twenty-six, Daisy, you're not almost anything."

"I'm on the wrong side of twenty-five, is what I am," I grumble and rub at my forehead with my fingertips. "When you're under twenty-five and your life goes to shit you can just shrug and be like, 'I'm only twenty-three.' Once you pass twenty-five..." I train off and shake my head. "Get it together, right? At a certain age it's just, this is your life. This is who you are." I throw my hands up to emphasize my point a moment before I remember he's almost forty and on a vacation courtesy of his grandmother. Awkward. "Sorry," I say. "I just feel like I'm running out of time."

"Daisy, you're twenty-six, not terminal."

"I suppose," I agree, but I smile because he's smiling and it's contagious.

"So what are you in a rush to accomplish then? What exactly is it you're running out of time on?"

I glance at him, wondering if I should continue. He still looks as though he's genuinely curious about what I have to say, so what the heck. I'm never going to see this guy again when the week is over and we're not in a relationship so there's no need to be politically correct.

"I'm going to be honest with you, Jennings."

"Please," he agrees, the hint of a smirk on his cheek.

I might as well be honest, since I'm lying to him about almost everything else. "Oh, by the way, I love carrot cake," I add as an afterthought. Daisy hates it—says carrots should only be consumed when dipped into ranch dressing.

"Carrot cake." He nods. "Noted. Thank you for being honest about that. It must have been quite difficult for you. Dicey topic and all."

"Hush, that was just a side note," I say, waving my hand. "I'm going to tell you something else."

"Please. I'm fascinated."

"I want to have a career and a family and sometimes I'm afraid I'm going to wake up at forty with neither." I glance in his direction. "No offense."

"Very well." He nods with that same smirk on his face. "None taken."

"You're a man so you have more time," I point out. "I'm sure it'll work out for you. I mean, assuming you want those things."

"The compliments just keep coming with you, don't they, love?"

"I just meant everyone has their own life path, you know? It's okay to be a free spirit. My sister is a free spirit. It works for some people, I'm just not one of them."

"Sure enough," he agrees. "So you think you're running out of time? Your biological clock is ticking, is it?"

"Oh!" I laugh. "No, not yet. Not ticking. I want to re-establish my career first. But I can see the clock, you know? I can't hear it ticking, but I'm aware that it's there. That it might need a battery at some point." I shrug before continuing. "It turns out that I've wasted the last couple of years and now I'm starting over. Which is fine, it just feels like the starting line got pushed back, that's all."

"Well, then," he says quietly. He looks pensive and I wonder if I really have just ensured I won't be coming again this week, which was so not my goal.

"No, I don't wish I could start over," he says after a moment. He slides his arm behind my headrest and leans in. "I'm good. I'm exactly where I'm meant to be. As are you."

CHAPTER FIFTEEN

Jennings

I am exactly where I'm meant to be. If I'd settled down earlier I wouldn't know how Daisy sounds when she comes. What she feels like wrapped around my cock. What she tastes like on my tongue. And not knowing those things? That's what regret would feel like.

Do I wish I'd settled down in my twenties and filled a nursery? Fuck no. I've still got time for all that. I'm youngish, loads of time. So what if I've worked hard and put family off? I've never questioned it before, yet suddenly this woman has me thinking. This woman who thinks I'm a free-spirited playboy with a dodgy career.

I might be guilty of one of those things. It's not as if I've ever had issues finding a woman to spend time with. But my career is solid—ten thousand employees rely on my career being solid—and I'm far from a free spirit. A structured workaholic is more like it. To a fault.

My parents had me just out of university, before my dad finished his legal training. Too young to my way of thinking. I was in short trousers by the time he qualified as a solicitor. A picture of me in one arm and his new practicing certificate in the other has been on his desk as long as I can remember. I used to look at it and think how exhausting it must have been to have a toddler at that stage in his life.

My mum must have agreed, because it was too much for her. The one who gave birth to me, not the one who raised me. My birth mum was gone before I was out of nappies. "She was too young to settle down," my dad would say when I asked about her, skipping over the fact that he was the same age. "She needed time to find herself." She found herself in Scotland, as it turned out. Married a Scotsman and had a couple of babies. Perhaps she was ready by then, as my half-sisters are both well over a decade younger than I am.

We did okay though by all accounts. Dad and I on our own. And then he met Elouise and she stepped in and became Mum. I'm not sure I remember a time before her. It's her I see in my childhood photos, a huge grin on her face as we posed in front of one tourist spot or another. Her soothing words I remember when I scraped my knee or broke a bone or lost a game. She's the only mum I've known and I'm okay with that. She really loves my dad. Must do, to have been so willing to accept me along with him.

So do I want a family of my own? Of course I do. Who doesn't? And having a family business does sort of require a family to pass it along to, doesn't it? Not that I don't have cousins who can take care of that. But I've got plenty of time. Loads.

No need to rush.

Daisy's got plans. Timelines. Goals. I'm a planner too—in business if not my personal life. It occurs to me now that I'll be forty in four years and this moment is the first time I've given it a second thought. Why has this girl who was supposed to be a one-off suddenly got me questioning my goals? I'd like to blame the memory of her on her knees with my cock in her mouth for my temporary insanity, but the truth is she's hypnotized me since the moment she gave me that shy smile at the hotel bar and then glanced away three seconds later. She's captured my attention more than I care to admit.

"I own a home," I tell her, and dammit if I don't sound a little sullen even to my own ears.

"You do?" She looks surprised. Likely because she thinks I'm some sort of jobless tosser living on contributions from my nan. I do own a home—a huge pile in one of the most expensive districts in London, bought for investment and location purposes as opposed to any actual need for it. I use one of the six bedrooms and bathrooms. I've never even sat in the formal dining room, choosing instead to eat at a stool at the kitchen island. The entire place could use a renovation but I've been loath to proceed. Loath because the space was more than I needed and I didn't want to bother customizing it for myself. I didn't see the need when I didn't have a family to fill it—a family there'd be plenty of time to have. Later.

"Yeah." I wave it off. "It's a fixer-upper." A fixer-upper with a current value of twelve million pounds. I paid under ten for it less than three years ago, but that's London for you. "Historic properties, you know how it is," I add so I don't sound like I'm living in a heap. I sound like a right wanker instead.

"Oh! I love old buildings!" Her entire face lights up at the mention. "I majored in urban planning but my focus was on honoring historic preservation while incorporating modern design. I'd have died to do an internship in Europe but I couldn't afford a semester overseas." She sighs before continuing. "Whenever I see an old building in disrepair I imagine what it must have looked like when it was built. And then I immediately envision its potential in today's age." She's talking with her hands and she pauses with one hand in front of her as if she's picturing a particularly enticing old pile of bricks. "What it would look like restored and how we'd use the space today. You're so lucky to live in a country with such a rich architectural history," she gushes. "When I see pictures of old European castles my mind races with ways to incorporate an HVAC system and how I'd retrofit bathrooms into the design. How I'd integrate a kitchen suitable for today with materials honoring the past." She sighs again when she's finished talking, a little smile on her lips as she daydreams about turning a dungeon into a wine cellar or some nonsense.

"So you're a designer? When you're not running tours?" I say because no, I've got no vision for piles of old rubble. When I see an old building, all I see are drafts and a bevy of maintenance costs. Issues with building regulations and delays on planning permission.

She snaps her mouth shut and flushes and it occurs to me that I might be coming across like a dick. Which wouldn't normally bother me, but I find that it does when it comes to Daisy. Her opinion matters to me more than it should. I can't figure her out—she glows when she talks design, and looks nothing short of uncomfortable when leading this tour. So why is she wasting her time on this job? Has she been unable to find employment in her chosen field? She must be several years out of university. It doesn't add up. She doesn't add up, yet with every word out of her mouth all I want to know is more. Anything more. Everything more.

She bites her lip and closes her eyes briefly before opening them again only to glance away. "I had a job in design, but the company was sold and my job was eliminated. It was mostly CAD work anyway, drafting the designs and schematics for the project managers. I didn't get to do much creatively."

"So you're working as a tour guide until something else comes up?" I ask. But that can't be right. She said she's worked at Sutton Travel for years. How was she doing this while also working at the design company that went under? The guide positions are by contract, meaning they work when they want to and based on tour schedules. But it still doesn't make sense.

"Um, I'm not sure," she murmurs but she's examining her fingernails instead of looking at me. "I mean sort of. Maybe."

"Perhaps you could move up within this company?" I suggest, ignoring her nonsensical answer. "This tour company is owned by a parent company, isn't it? With hotels and the like, surely. They must have designers on staff to handle the acquisitions and remodels."

She looks at me, interest sparking briefly in her eyes before it disappears just as quickly. I wonder if I've overstepped the line. Then she frowns, tiny lines appearing on her forehead before she's rising in her seat and slipping past me into the aisle. "I've got to prep the group for Mount Vernon," she states without looking at me, but I'm not sure if that's true or if she's just looking for a way to end this conversation. A conversation that's left me with more questions than answers.

I watch as Daisy turns on the microphone and grabs the group's attention. Then she reiterates that we're on our way to Mount Vernon—the same information she gave them when the bus left the hotel not twenty minutes ago. I tap my finger on my mobile while I try to recall the time difference between the East Coast and Las Vegas.

I think it's time to start digging.

CHAPTER SIXTEEN

Violet

I'm the worst. Literally the worst. My pulse is racing so fast. Why did I just tell him all that? It's a good thing no one's life depends on my ability to lie because I suck at it. I suck all the sucks. That sounds sorta perverted, doesn't it? Perfect, now I'm thinking about sucking his dick.

It's a nice dick. A great one, really. I smile thinking about my naïveté regarding uncut cocks. I can't believe I told him I didn't know what to do with it. I'm so ridiculous. It was basically the same, except easier to give him a hand job. And more sensitive. Like when I swirled my tongue around the head and he made that little groaning noise that almost made *me* come. I swear groans in British sound different than American ones. Like a way better kind of different, which sounds crazy but I promise is true.

I take a huge breath and try to calm myself as I grab the microphone so I can repeat the same information I gave the group twenty minutes ago. Information that doesn't need to be repeated, but I needed to get away from Jennings. Granted, I've only managed to get two feet away from him, but I'll take it.

I can't believe I just word-vomited out all that information about myself, but it's not like he's going to check, right? It's not like he would know what Daisy majored in or what she does when she's not on tours. It's not like he has access to her employment files to verify anything I just told him. I almost laugh out loud at the idea. Can I be any more paranoid?

He knows nothing.

Nada.

Zip.

Zilch.

I like him.

Wait. Where did that thought come from? I glance over my shoulder to where he's sitting, still next to the seat I just escaped from. His head is bent over his phone and he appears to be tapping out a text or an email. From this angle I can see his jaw ticking in concentration as he types.

So of course I like him. I'm sleeping with him and it's not as if I go around sleeping with men I don't like. I liked the look of him when I smiled at him in the bar that first night, didn't I? I liked his eyes. And his jaw. His dark hair and the way his shirt fit his shoulders. I liked that he sent me a drink when all I did was offer up that stupid three-second smile. No one's ever sent me a drink before. In the movies men are always sending drinks, but in reality it doesn't happen that often. At least not in my reality. In college I had guys offer me red Solo cups filled with beer from the keg, but it's not the same thing.

I like the tone of his voice and his British accent. I like the way he smells and the feel of him pressed against me.

It's just the sex, right?

Except I like the way he pays attention when I talk. The way he wants to know more—even though I can't tell him more because I'm a big fat liar. But nonetheless, I like the way he pays attention. It was sweet how he suggested I look for openings within the company. It wouldn't be a terrible idea, if I actually worked for the company. Daisy isn't qualified for positions I'd be interested in, not to mention it would be problematic to apply as her and keep this charade running any longer. I'm still not convinced I'll make it to the end of this tour without blowing it.

But I could have Daisy keep an eye out for the jobs I'd be qualified for and then apply for those as myself, couldn't I? Daisy'd probably even get a bonus for referring me. Wouldn't that be something? She dumps her job on me and then ends up getting a bonus out of it. Quintessentially Daisy.

I like the way Jennings keeps an eye on his nan and makes sure she's got everything she needs. How he always exits the bus ahead of her so he can hold her arm as she takes the last step from the bus to the pavement.

I like the way he watches me when I'm fumbling through this tour, a look of curiosity on his face as if I'm more interesting than I actually am.

I also like the way he looks at me when we're having sex. The way his eyes stay on mine when he thrusts into me. The way he cups my chin and moves my gaze back to his when I've turned my head away. How he touches me and—enough. It's the best sex I've ever had. I know it's cliché and semi-dramatic, but it's that good. And maybe twice doesn't exactly equal a case study, but it's enough of a sample to make a pretty good argument in his favor. Dammit, why does it have to be so good? It's making me feel things, things I have no business feeling.

So what if I like him? It's not a big deal. It's just a week. My perfect one-night stand turned into the perfect one-week fling. It's what I wanted, isn't it? A no-strings-attached liaison to help me get back in the game. A rebound relationship, so to speak. One I should have had six months ago to get my ex out of my system. Because it totally worked. Maybe it's the time that's passed or maybe it's Jennings, but I can honestly say I've moved on. I feel hopeful. I feel glad—well, almost—that my last company went under because it forced me to face that neither my job or my relationship were a good fit. I couldn't see it for myself so fate stepped in and forced me to.

Just like fate is going to force this thing I have with Jennings to an end when the tour ends. So I like him. So what? There's no crime in liking your temporary lover. When I remember this week it will be filled with happy memories. Torrid, scandalous memories. Sinful, dirty recollections of brown eyes, perfect abs and sly smiles that wet my panties and restored my confidence.

No big deal.

The bus pulls onto the Mount Vernon grounds, so I snap myself out of my lewd musings and focus on recalling how Daisy handled this part of the tour. The group is taking the premium mansion tour, which is led by someone who is not me, thank goodness. I've just got to run into the tour office and coordinate handing the group off.

Twenty minutes later I've instructed the group where the meeting point is once their guided tour is over, with free time added in order for them to explore the grounds on their own. Then I sigh the happiest sigh of relief as I watch the group depart without me, Jennings along with them. I've got three hours of freedom. Three hours in which I won't accidentally tell Jennings too much. Three hours in which I won't be swayed by his accent, by his brown eyes, by the way he draws me into telling him too much.

He's just a fun distraction—and that's great. But a week from now he'll be gone so I need to keep it together. I don't need to fall for him. And I don't need to blow my sister's job and lose this week's paycheck because of my big mouth.

What I need to do is focus on the future. On finding a new job, a new place to live. On getting my life back on track. Not on falling for someone I can't be with. Not to mention—he's not even my type. I go for goal-oriented men. Suits. Mr. Casual Concert T-shirt is so not my type.

CHAPTER SEVENTEEN

Jennings

"What exactly do you need to know and why can't you ask her yourself?"

I've put in a call to my cousin Rhys. My American cousin, younger by two years. His mother is my father's sister. She grew up in England but left when she fell for a foreign exchange student during university—and followed him home. All the way home to Connecticut. Somehow Rhys and I have always been close despite growing up on different continents. It helped that once we were old enough we spent summers together, alternating between the US and the UK each year. Looking back I suspect our parents made this deal to buy themselves a kid-free summer every other year, but the end result is that it made Rhys and I thick as thieves.

"It's complicated," I reply and it makes me smile. I sound like Daisy with her evasive excuses.

"What do you mean it's complicated? Didn't you introduce yourself? We don't *Undercover Boss* the employees, Jennings. That's policy. Senior-level employees introduce themselves whether they're traveling on company or personal business. We don't hoodwink the employees."

"Hoodwink? Really, Rhys?"

"It's a word, asshole. Stop avoiding the question."

"I would've," I tell him, "but I'd already met her. The night prior. And then things got... complicated." There's that word again.

There's a brief pause while he takes that in. I hear him stop typing and imagine he's settled back into his chair so he can focus on giving me shit.

"You British bastard. You have all the goddamned luck, don't you? When I took Nan on a tour of the Canadian Rockies last year our guide was a fifty-year-old-man named Marvin."

"Sorry, Rhys." I grin even though he can't see it. "I do have a rather lucky way with the breaks, don't I?"

"Asshole."

"Plus I'm older, better-looking and better at sport than you."

"Better at sport," he mocks. "You're such a British wanker. Better at cricket, maybe. And you're nowhere near as good-looking as me. Everyone knows I'm the best-looking of the cousins."

"Everyone knows? You've taken a poll, have you?"

"I heard it discussed at Christmas. Uncle David's new wife mentioned it."

"She did not." I snort.

"She thought it though," he replies, undeterred. "In any case, you're taking Nan next year too. This trip doesn't count as a turn if you're banging the tour guide."

"Deal. And don't be crass, Rhys, Daisy's not a showgirl."

"There's not a showgirl in sight," he says easily.

"Of course not."

"And they prefer to be called entertainers."

"There you have it. Difficult life you lead in the desert, Rhys," I deadpan. He's currently in Las Vegas overseeing the newest acquisition for the family business, Sutton

International—the opening of a two-billion-dollar hotel and casino on the Vegas strip.

"I don't have access to the employee files in the tour division," he finally says. "Isn't this the shit? Who do I need to fuck around here to get clearance?"

"Likely a relative, so you might want to reconsider that."

"Shit. Way to ruin that fantasy, asshole." I hear him tapping again at his keyboard before announcing that he's sent a request to the casino's human resources director. "She'll either have access to all the US employment files or know who does. I'll get the file sent over to you as soon as I have it," he says.

"Thanks, Rhys."

"No worries. It's not as if we're in the midst of hiring and training four thousand employees in time for the opening."

"Appreciate it," I drawl as I walk through the garden of the George Washington estate. I ditched the group once we were through the orientation area, Nan happily waving me off when I told her I had calls to make.

Rhys and I both work for the family business—the one founded by Nan's father some sixty years past. This makes us the fourth generation of family members involved in the running of Sutton International, parent company to a hotel group, river cruise line and three brands of bus tours. Including the one I'm on right now.

We have offices on six continents and offer holidays to over two hundred destinations worldwide. Rhys is heading up the Vegas project while another cousin presides over our business in Canada. An uncle runs the river cruise division out of an office in Switzerland.

And me? I'm responsible for overseeing all of it.

"What is it you need anyway?" Rhys interrupts my

thoughts. "You want her phone number? Date of birth? Home address? Because you could save all of us a lot of trouble and just ask her yourself."

"I'm curious. I need more information."

"That you can't get from her."

"That's right." The gravel below my feet crunches as I walk and I smile at this mini-inquisition from Rhys.

"Are you sure this girl is even interested in you?"

"She's interested."

"What's wrong with her?"

"Nothing is wrong with her. She's quite lovely. Possibly a pathological liar, but lovely." I look up to find the woman herself standing not ten feet away. She too is on her mobile and spots me the same time I spot her. She takes a half step back, keeping her eyes on me as she talks. I take a step to the left, avoiding a small child running full tilt through the garden, and adding an additional step between myself and Daisy.

"She sounds interesting," Rhys says into my ear, amusement clear in his tone.

"Oh, she is," I agree as Daisy and I continue to eye each other across the garden. Clearly neither of us is interested in the other overhearing their conversation. She turns and walks down a graveled path until we're separated by a large planting bed filled with an ornate pattern of shrubbery, both of us continuing our conversations with the other in view. "She most certainly is that."

"You like her," Rhys says slowly, dragging the words out as if the concept is new to him.

"I'm enjoying myself. That's all." A breeze passes through the garden, ruffling the hem of Daisy's sundress. It's pale yellow, ending a couple of inches above her knees. My eyes travel lower, down her tan calves to her sandal-clad feet and back up again. She's pulling a strand of hair from her lipstick and ignoring me.

"Good. It's about time."

"What's that supposed to mean?" I stop walking and examine a flowering ornamental tree of some sort while keeping Daisy in sight.

"Sperm mobility decreases with age. It might already be too late for you."

"Jesus Christ," I mutter.

"The family line is depending on you."

"Stop taking the piss out of me, cuz. You're only two years younger than me and I don't see you planning your nursery."

"Planning my nursery?" He laughs. "This British shit never gets old and I've known you my whole life."

"Yes, your American colloquialisms continue to delight me as well, Rhys."

"I'm sure. So are you headed straight back to London after the tour or can you squeeze in a visit to Vegas?"

"I'm delivering Nan to your mother in Bethany first, then yes, back to London. I'm a bit pressed for time with everything going on at the office."

"You're always pressed for time," Rhys points out. It's true. I feel like I'm constantly on the go. I like that though, don't I?

The company keeps me busy. Nepotism will get you in the door and, yes, it will quicken your path of promotional opportunities but you've still got to do the work. Earn your place. Or there'll be no company for the next generation of children and our ten thousand worldwide employees will be without jobs.

Children I may not have at the rate my personal life is moving. And if Rhys is to be believed about my declining virility.

So no pressure. None at all. The hallway to my office is lined with photographical evidence of over fifty years in business. Fifty years of growth and acquisitions. Of success and new job creation. Of bonuses being paid and benefits increased. Of ancestors staring at me from those photographs, wordlessly imploring me not to bugger it all to hell now.

Easy.

My father skipped the family business—initially. His passion was law, so he pursued that. Had a very successful career in criminal law before making the switch to corporate law when he joined the family business. He's the head of legal now but has his eye on retiring in the next couple of years. My cousin Mila is poised to take over that team when the time comes.

"We've made a lot of progress since you were last here. We've taken ownership of the residential floors and the director-level employees have already moved on site. I'll set you up in a suite on property and you can see the progress in person. We'll even watch the showgirls rehearse for the opening," Rhys teases.

"We'll see," I tell him. My focus is back on the beauty across the garden.

"I've got to let you go. I've got a meeting with the city in ten minutes. But consider it, Jennings. You can bring your new friend. I'd love to meet her."

"I bet you would. I suspect you and Daisy would get on quite well." They both seem to enjoy giving me shit.

"You might want to tell her who you are first," he adds.

"I might," I agree. "I just need to figure her out first."

"Sure, keep lying. That usually works with women."

Fuck. I pause for a moment, thinking about what he's said. He's got a point, hasn't he?

"I'm in a bit too deep, aren't I?"

"Most definitely," he agrees with a laugh. "Keep me updated. I'll forward her file when I've got it."

"Thanks, Rhys."

I disconnect the call and pocket my mobile. Daisy is still in the same spot.

I did a few of these tours myself, back when I was starting out with the company, just out of university. Not in the United States of course—the guides are meant to be regional experts and local to the country. The majority of my family started out the same way—either as tour guides or in entry-level positions at one of the hotels.

So I did a six-month stint of the Glorious Britain tour and another six with the Highlights of the United Kingdom tour before I got my first position in the London office. That was more years ago than I care to recall. Rhys's words regarding my schedule echo in my head. I've heard similar words from my father.

I've never had a reason to slow down. Not a compelling reason.

Another breeze passes through the garden, causing Daisy's dress to billow in a way that makes her look pregnant.

My cock hardens.

Jesus Christ, am I disturbed or having some kind of normal prehistoric reaction to the idea of her with child? This is fucked. I've never reacted like this before to the idea of a pregnant woman. Or is it to the idea of impregnating her? Bloody hell.

Rhys is messing with my head, is all. Bloody sperm mobility; I shake my head and smile. What an arsehole. Pulling the mobile from my pocket, I thumb open the contacts until I find who I'm looking for and hit dial.

Across the garden Daisy struggles with another strand

of hair in her lipstick. She pauses next to a bench and drops her trusty notebook before perching on the edge of the bench beside it. I see her gesturing with her free hand for a moment before setting the phone down face up on the bench, then she's sliding an elastic off her wrist and gathering her long dark hair back, the movements reminding me of her on her knees before me as she gathered her hair in preparation for sucking my cock.

The memory does nothing to help with the swelling in my trousers. I wonder if I'm now conditioned to get a hard-on every time she pulls her hair into a pony and I'm unsure if that's a blessing or a curse. A bit of both, perhaps.

"Hey, Jennings, how's the tour?" My call has connected. It's Priscilla in the London office.

"Very well. Listen, I need you to do something for me." I turn from Daisy as I talk, examining the windows on the stately greenhouse as I proceed to outline what I need from Priscilla. I wonder what Daisy thinks when she looks at this building. If the brick is to her liking, if she marvels at the ingenuity in design. If she's contemplating how she'd retrofit it into condominiums or a mini-mart.

"You're handing over the Leo project? In its entirety?" Priscilla questions when I'm done speaking. Rightfully so, because delegation isn't my strongest suit. Or it hasn't been.

"Yes. You're more than ready to lead a project of this scope without me. I have complete confidence in you." It's true. I can't recall a recommendation she's made that I've disagreed with. She's more than fit for the task. And it's time I started delegating because that's the bloody point, isn't it? To hire and develop the best talent so they can do the job you've hired them for. It's part of our corporate philosophy, one I could do a better job adhering to. Cultivating existing talent so that good employees become great and the great ones soar.

I end the call satisfied I've sorted that and contemplate my next move.

Then I close the distance between me and Daisy. She tilts her head to the side as I approach, still on the phone, a now-familiar look of skepticism crossing her face. I think she reserves that look for me and I find that I like it. I like that she isn't polite with me, she's real. What you see is what you get. Minus all the lies coming out of her mouth, that is. But I'll figure those out soon enough. I stop in front of her and grin, my plan set.

She looks up at me, saying nothing. I assume whomever she's speaking with is still on the line because she hasn't taken the phone from her ear, silently appraising me while listening.

"I've got to go," she says into the phone, her eyes still on mine. She listens for another moment, then if I'm not mistaken says, "You're my cracker," and hangs up.

"You're supposed to be on a tour with the others." She doesn't seem amused with me at present, eyeing me warily while capping her pen and dropping it along with her notebook into her bag.

"Mandatory, is it?"

"Well, it's preferred." She crosses her legs and I'm momentarily distracted by the movement—one slim calf resting against the other, her knee visible as the sundress she's wearing settles a few inches above. She rests against the back of the bench and bounces her foot. "So I can keep tabs on you. You're like a cat. Always popping up when I least expect you."

I laugh. I'm certain no one's ever described me as such before.

"Actually, that's not fair." She frowns. "I like cats and

they're very rarely sneaky. They're too lethargic to be sneaky most of the time."

"So you don't like me?"

"I do like you. It was a bad analogy all the way around." She shakes her head then pauses. "Wait." She grins and snaps her fingers. "I've got it. Spy!" She laughs, seemingly amused with herself. "You're more like a spy. You'd be great undercover. Very stealthy. You should look into it."

"I'll give it some serious consideration."

She leans forward on the bench and holds up her hand in the universal stop motion, as if it's important she makes this distinction. "Don't get me wrong. A hot spy. More James Bond than Austin Powers. It'd be sexy if I enjoyed being spied on."

Right. Rhys' *Undercover Boss* comment rings in my ear and I feel abashed for lying to her. Yet what has she got to hide? Isn't that really the question? I know she's lying about something. She's a hot mess of contradictions and things that don't add up. If I had any sense at all I'd be doing the exact opposite of what I'm about to do, but bloody feelings are the antonym of sense.

My phone buzzes with an incoming call from London. I glance at it before sending it to voicemail so I can focus on the task at hand.

"Normally I'd ask if you were free tonight, but we both already know that you are, so I'll cut right to the chase. I'd like to take you on a date tonight."

"A date?" The skepticism I've come to associate with her is back in a blink as a hint of confusion crosses her face.

"Dinner," I clarify, as it seems she's not comprehending. "A proper date."

"Oh." Her brows rise as her lips form the word and

the skepticism on her face morphs into curiosity.

I wait, expecting her to say something. Something like yes, but she's silent. I'm not sure what the hell she's thinking about, her head tilted to the side while she stares at me and thinks. Fuck me, she's cute. She's stunning, really. But it's these little moments that charm me. When she drops all pretenses, unworried about impressing me. When she scrunches her nose or rolls her eyes or makes me wait far too long for an answer.

"Eight o'clock, then?" I tell her, because fuck it, she's going to dinner with me. I'm not taking no for an answer.

"Why?" she asks, without a hint of playing coy.

"Why?" I laugh and shake my head. What does she mean, why? I remind myself she's a bit younger than me and wonder if dating has completely gone to hell in the decade that separates us or if this kind of a response is simply Daisy. My phone buzzes again. I don't even look at it as I turn the ringer to silent and wonder how I've made it this far without the amusement of a woman requesting I justify why I want to take her on a date.

"Because we like each other and it will be fun. Because we haven't had a proper first date and you deserve one. Because I enjoy spending time with you."

"Okay." She nods her head once in agreement and I think that's settled. Then she opens her mouth again to provide a list of reasons why I shouldn't pick her up at the door.

I really, really like her.

CHAPTER EIGHTEEN

Violet

A date.

He asked me on a date. After eye-fucking me across the garden and distracting me from my call—which was a total bust—he asked me to go on a date with him.

I stared at him, suspicious about what he was up to, because who asks a sure thing to go on a date? What is the point in that? A sure thing means you eat a quick sandwich by yourself, brush your teeth and then meet up somewhere for sex. At least I think that's what it means. I've never really done this before but dinner seems unnecessary. I was staring at him trying to figure out if he'd meant dinner or if 'date' was British slang for sex when he smiled and tossed in the phrase, "A proper date."

For the love of all that is holy, why is the word 'proper' a turn-on? Because it is, at least when spoken by Mr. Sexy Voice. Then I started daydreaming about how I was going to get a voice recording of him saying 'proper' before the week was up so I could play it on repeat after he was gone. Which led to the super-genius idea of developing vibrators that speak dirty to you in a British accent, which was interrupted by Jennings saying, "Earth to Daisy," and snapping me out of contemplating what the overhead costs would be to get something like that in development.

Once he had my attention he asked again to take me to dinner. "A proper date, love. I'll take you to dinner and walk you to your door. Tonight," he added while doing that eye-fucking thing again.

So I think he meant both dinner and sex.

I'm free tonight. A fact Jennings pointed out because he'd taken the time to check the itinerary and confirm that there's no group dinner planned for the tour this evening.

You know what rebounds are good for? Rebounding. They are not meant to make you fall for them before they go home. To a place that you couldn't even drive to if you hypothetically wanted to see them again because an ocean separates your countries. International flights for booty calls seem really impractical.

Groaning, I pull back the duvet covering my bed so I can flop onto it. We arrived in Williamsburg about an hour ago but I'm just now walking into my room. The check-in process is fairly seamless as we're pre-checked in at each hotel by the tour company, but I'm responsible for getting the keys from reception and then handing them off to each guest while they hover around me anxious to get up to their rooms. And then there's the questions. *Does this hotel have a pool? What time is breakfast? When does the bus leave in the morning? Where can I buy a magnet that says Williamsburg, Virginia? Where should I eat dinner tonight? Is it safe to walk? Is there free wifi in this hotel? Is there a Wal-Mart close by?*

Who the heck comes to America to see a Wal-Mart?

In any case, I'm finally done doing Daisy's job for the day and blissfully alone. Which gives me time to think.

Dinner seems like it involves feelings. My feelings.

I eye the ceiling for another minute then thumb my

phone to life and place a call.

"Please tell me you're calling to talk about your new British lover, because I cannot handle any more bitching about the tour," Daisy says by way of hello.

"Hello to you too," I deadpan.

"Hey, girl, hey," she replies. "Is that better?" There's a buzzing or some noise in the background I can't identify.

"What is that noise? Is that your vibrator?"

"What? No, you freaking weirdo," she says slowly, "it's the microwave."

"Sorry," I tell her. "It sounded like a vibrator."

"I'm happy to know you think I'm unable to stop vibing long enough to answer the phone."

"Vibing? Is that a word?"

"It is now. So what's up?"

"I'm, uh, calling to talk to you about my new British lover."

"Did we really just go through that entire song and dance when I was correct to begin with?"

"Yes," I admit. "The tour went well today though, thanks for asking."

"Glad to hear it," she says easily as the microwave beeps.

"I'm still never doing this again. Ever. Ever, ever," I repeat because I'm not sure she's taking me seriously. "So you'd better be back from whatever it is you're doing in time for the next tour. I mean it."

"Never, ever," she agrees. "No more tours. Now tell me about your guy."

"Tell me where you are. Because that was not your microwave. Yours beeps differently," I add with a triumphant finger pointed at the ceiling. I know she can't see it but it still feels good to have sleuthed that out.

"Mad detective work," she quips. "I'm visiting a

friend."

"A friend? What friend?" That's so not an answer. Everyone's Daisy's friend. A friend could be some guy she met twenty-seven minutes ago or a classmate from first grade.

"Fine. More of a frenemy," she admits as she stuffs something into her mouth.

"A frenemy with benefits?" I question.

"It's complicated," she mutters around a mouthful of food and I smile. We're definitely twins. "I'll tell you about it later when it makes more sense," she adds.

"So you're hate-fucking some guy all week while I do your job? Is that what's happening here?"

"You're not exactly suffering, Vi. Now why don't you tell me about Mr. Tall, Dark and British and stop harassing me?"

"Fine." I sigh loudly and dramatically into the phone. "He's nice," I finally say after a long pause.

"He's nice?" Daisy repeats, her tone making clear how she feels about that summary. "That's why you're calling me? Because he's nice?"

"Sorta," I admit. It does sound pretty stupid when I say it out loud.

"Weren't you just bragging to me about how great the sex is? Like, the last time I talked to you which was all of six hours ago? What the hell happened in the last six hours?"

"I was not bragging!"

"You so were," she replies, unfazed. "Honestly, I was proud of you."

"Oh. Well, thank you. I think."

"You're welcome. So what's the problem? Is he boring?"

"Erm..." I can see where this is confusing. "No, he's

not boring. Not at all. He makes me laugh."

"Are you bipolar or something? Is that hereditary? I can't deal with this right now," she mutters and I hear the clang of dinnerware as she sets down whatever she's eating. "So he's hot, he's nice and he makes you laugh. Is he dumb? Is that the problem? Sometimes the pretty ones aren't the brightest. I know it's not politically correct to say so, but it is what it is. But it's just a week, it's not like you're having his baby, so just let it go and have fun."

"I like him," I blurt out. "Okay? The problem is I like him."

"Oh." Daisy's quiet for a moment while she takes that in. "And you're worried you're going to fall in love with him and have dumb children? I just saw this little monster of a child at Target and he was screaming his head off asking for glue. Glue! What kind of kid asks for glue? I suspect—"

"Daisy." I cut her off mid-sentence. "He's not dumb. Can you focus, please? He's not dumb and we're not having children."

"You never know," she huffs. "Shit happens."

"Focus," I repeat.

"Okay, okay. So what exactly is the problem? He's hot. Good in bed. Smart. Nice. Makes you laugh and you like him. This is you living your best life."

"He asked me to have dinner with him."

"Yeah, that sounds like a huge problem. Wear my navy dress. The one with the lace hem. I know I packed it."

"It's just..." I start and stop, trying to put what I'm feeling into words. "It's just that he was supposed to be a one-night stand, not make me fall for him."

"Take it from me, a lot of things happen that aren't supposed to."

"Was that meant to be reassuring?"

"Listen to me, Vi, I've dated a lot of guys, most of them assholes."

This is true.

"So when life hands you a good one, grab him."

She's got a point.

"And then get him microchipped so you always know where he is."

"Daisy," I groan.

"Violet." Her voice softens. "None of this is a problem, trust me. This is the fun stuff. Go to dinner. Have fun. Screw his brains out. You'll figure the rest out later. Or he'll annoy the shit out of you before the week is over and the rest won't matter."

"Sage advice," I say, but I'm smiling. I can always count on her to call it like it is.

"I know," she agrees. "Someone should hire me to write greeting cards."

"They should."

"Remember, sometimes the best things in life are unplanned."

"Just like twins. I love you. You're my cupcake."

"Love you too, sprinkles. Now go have fun. And wear the navy dress!"

CHAPTER NINETEEN

Violet

I hang up with Daisy and jump into the shower because if I'm going on a date I might as well primp. I think about what Daisy said as I towel-dry. She's got some valid points. I've planned my entire life and where did it get me? Heartbroken and homeless, that's where.

Meanwhile Daisy flies by the seat of her pants and always manages to land on her feet. More than land on her feet, really. She's totally got her shit together. Dumping her job on me to meet up with some guy for a hate-fuck not withstanding.

The call today with the recruiter was a total bust—I'd been hoping she was calling with an opportunity. Turns out she was only calling to check if I'm certified in Revit. I'm not. My experience is entirely with AutoCAD design, which is fine because Revit is for dweebs who do nothing but yell at people when they use the wrong title block.

But it sucked getting my hopes up. For the hour or so until I was able to call the recruiter back hope swirled around in my stomach—hope that this could be the lead I've been waiting for. I even had a little fantasy that the job would require overseas trips to London and Jennings would invite me over to his place and we'd order takeout and have sex. Obviously that was a really specific and unlikely fantasy but fantasies are by definition improbable.

I pull the navy dress out of my suitcase because Daisy's right about that too. It's a great dress and it looks fantastic on Daisy, which by default means it's going to look fantastic on me. One of the biggest benefits of being a twin is having a built-in fit model.

I am sort of surprised she lent it to me though, it's one of her favorites. She packed a lot of great outfits for me this week, which was sweet of her. It's not that I don't have clothes of my own, it's just that my wardrobe leans towards professional, whereas hers leans towards Pinterest board goals.

But it was nice of her because in sisterhood nothing says 'I love you' quite like lending your favorite dress.

I blow-dry my hair and use a wide-barreled curling iron to add a few casual tousled waves, the kind of casual that you put a lot of effort into. I keep my eye on the clock as I get ready because Jennings is picking me up. I told him I'd meet him in the lobby and he insisted that on a proper first date he'd pick me up at the door.

I told him that on a real first date I'd never let him pick me up at the door because he could be a serial killer. Or possibly just an annoying asshole who I wouldn't want having my address. Or maybe the date would be so painfully bad that I'd have to bail early by secretly texting a friend to call me with a fake emergency and then I'd need my own car to get the hell out of there.

He stared at me without saying anything for a moment, his head tilted to the side and his fingers running across his jaw. Then we agreed that I'd overlook my normal first-date protocols this time, which is just as well because I don't have sex on first dates either and I have no intention of sticking to that rule tonight.

I slide my feet into my favorite pair of sandals and am

sliding earrings on when Jennings knocks at the door. I grin, suddenly stupid excited about tonight. It's been forever since I went on a date with someone new and my stomach is filled with unexpected butterflies as I swing open the door. Butterflies that don't settle when I see him. He's showered as well, his hair clearly the slightest bit damp. He's in another button-down shirt, which I haven't seen him in since the first night. This one is white, the sleeves rolled back to mid-forearm, which I notice immediately because one arm is braced against the doorway and the other hand is holding flowers.

"Roses," he says, holding them up. "I was going to get you daisies but then I figured every guy brings you daisies, but how many men can you possibly have given the alias Rose to?" He winks at me when he says it, confident that Rose is our thing, that I don't go around giving out fake names to men. He's correct.

"I'm glad they're not daisies," I tell him as I take them from his hand, almost laughing at the idea that every guy brings me flowers. My high-school boyfriend would buy me a single rose whenever there was a school fundraiser. Student council would deliver them to classrooms during second period and the girls would carry them from class to class for the remainder of the day. I'm sure if I opened an old yearbook I'd find one still pressed inside. One time I got a delivery at work from my ex. It was my birthday and I'm pretty sure he ordered them that morning for same-day delivery from a local florist because he'd forgotten, but it was still nice. But a parade of flowers? No.

He's also correct about the daisies—Daisy has received them an unseemly number of times and she loves them, but they're her, not me. Of course Jennings can't know that, but I'm grateful that he thought of the roses. That he picked out something specific to the two of us. The last thing I'd have wanted was a bouquet of daisies staring me in the face reminding me of my big fat lie.

"They're perfect, thank you," I tell him as I grab the hotel-provided ice bucket and fill it with a few inches of water in the bathroom sink. I set it next to the television and stick the flowers inside. It's not the right kind of container and they sort of slump to the side and yet it's perfect. Perfectly imperfect.

"Ready?" he asks, but he's directly behind me, running a fingertip down the exposed side of my neck. I shiver and turn to face him.

"I'm ready."

"You look smashing, love." He says it softly, his eyes dancing over my face, and I think he's going to kiss me—he's standing so close I can feel the heat of his body—but he simply takes my hand and leads me to the door. We hold hands all the way to the elevator, our fingers entwined and my pulse racing. I'm not entirely sure why. He's not exactly new to me and this isn't a real first date. It's a third or fourth date at least, isn't it? God, how many days ago was that first night? How is it that I already feel like I've known him forever? How have I forgotten a world before Jennings in less than a week? I'm tumbling head over heels like a foolish puppy tripping over its own feet.

Or a fool falling in love when this relationship has an expiration date shorter than the date on a carton of milk.

Is this real? Or an illusion brought on by close quarters and explosive chemistry? It's so easy between us, but is it easy because it's temporary? A trip to an amusement park is exhilarating for a day or two, but it would be a nightmare if you went every single day for an entire year, wouldn't it? I bite my bottom lip and glance at him under my lashes. The elevator doors slide open and our hands part as we enter and he jabs the button for the lobby.

"What's going on in that head of yours, love?" His head is tilted and one brow raised in question and I wonder how he knows to ask me this based on one quiet walk down a hallway.

"I was just wondering if you like amusement parks." Close enough.

"Is that a hard limit for you? Whether or not your dates enjoy the Tilt-A-Whirl?" His response is light, but I caught the quick blink that tells me he didn't buy my response to his question.

"I like them, but I tend to get motion-sick after a couple of rides," I admit with a shrug. Is this a metaphor for my love life as well? Get in and out before anyone gets dizzy? "I never get sick of the arcade games or the cotton candy though."

"If it's not a deal-breaker, then I'll admit theme parks aren't my first choice of holiday. Of course, I'd never have picked a tour of American historic sites either and it's turning out to be far more"—he pauses and eyes me slowly—"lively than I'd expected."

I blush. He has a way of making a simple response sound indecent. I clear my throat before speaking. "What would your preference have been?"

"When I have the time? Skiing."

"I've never been skiing."

"No?" He glances at me and starts to say something then stops. I wonder if he's stopping himself from making a throwaway comment about the future such as, *We should go sometime.*

We've exited the lobby of the hotel and I expect to get

into a cab, but he guides me towards a waiting black SUV, so I assume he's called an Uber. I guess this means we're not going to the pancake house across the street, which makes me giggle.

Jennings slides into the back of the SUV after me and takes my hand, kissing the back of it. "Something funny?"

I tap my finger against the window in the direction of the International House of Pancakes across the street. "IHOP," I tell him. "It's a chain restaurant. When we were kids my sister called it 'I Jump' till we were like…" I stop. I can't tell him we're the same age, that's way too much information. "Till she was like seven," I finish. "That's a stupid story. I don't know why I told it to you."

"It's not a stupid story. I enjoyed hearing it. Are you close with your sister?"

You could say that, since we're identical twins and I'm wearing her clothes and living in her apartment. "She's my other half. Do you have any siblings?"

"Two half-sisters. I don't really know them. We grew up in different households and they're much younger than I am. They were raised in Scotland. I've only met them a handful of times actually."

"I'm sorry."

"Why? Scotland is lovely. It's hardly a tragic situation."

"No." I laugh. "No offense to Scotland. I meant I was sorry you weren't closer with your sisters. I can't imagine life without my sister."

"Yeah, well. It is what it is." He runs a hand over his jaw but otherwise doesn't give away if this is something that bothers him. "I've a cousin I'm close with. He's like a brother to me. You'd like him, I think. He's got your American sense of humor."

"Your cousin is American?" I twist in my seat so I can see him. "How does that happen?"

He laughs as the car pulls onto Richmond and accelerates through a green light. "You need me to explain the basics to you, love? You seem a smart girl."

"No." I thump his chest with my palm. "I just meant my entire family lives in Illinois. My parents. My sister. Aunts, uncles, grandparents. One cousin moved to Pittsburgh and another moved to Orlando but everyone else is nearby. It's not as though I have a random German cousin."

"Wow. You let me pick you up at the door *and* disclosed which state you live in. I'm feeling quite chuffed."

"Don't get overconfident. I can still fake an emergency and take a cab back to the hotel."

"Duly noted. I'll do my best to entertain you well enough that you don't need to pull a runner."

"Naperville, Illinois," I offer because there can't be much harm in telling him that much. "I'm from a city called Naperville. It's a suburb of Chicago and it's very... suburban," I offer for lack of a better description. I try to picture bumping into a guy like Jennings living in Naperville and find that I can't. If I could find a guy like Jennings in Naperville he'd already have a wife and two kids. They'd have a Bugaboo stroller for the toddler and the baby would be strapped to his chest in a Tula and they'd have a nice house within walking distance of the riverwalk and I'd hate them a little.

"My aunt Poppy married an American. Their children were born and raised in the US," he explains. "I've got relatives all over though. It's fairly normal in our family, I suppose."

"But you're close with your cousin?" I question. "Growing up so far apart?"

"We spent summers together. Alternated between the

UK and the US."

"Huh," I say, not attempting to be subtle. The car makes another turn and I wonder where it is we're going. I squint out the window, trying to place us. I think the tour bus was on this road earlier.

"Dare I ask?" He sounds amused and I bring my eyes back to his.

"I was just imagining you visiting during your teenage years…" I trail off while resting a hand on his knee.

"And?"

"And I'm thinking about all those American girls who didn't know what to do with it." My voice is soft and neutral given we're not alone in the car, but I slide my hand higher as I speak.

In retrospect it might have been more effective if I'd been bold enough to go farther than mid-thigh, because instead of being seduced Jennings laughs.

"Are you still thinking about that?" He places his hand on top of mine and runs the pad of his thumb softly over the back of my hand. I think he's done more to seduce me with this one simple unthought move than I did with my intentional slide up his leg.

"No…" I draw the word out. Maybe. A little bit. Yes. The answer is yes.

"Are you jealous, love?"

"No!" I scoff. "Of course not." I shake my head a little. "But I mean, how big is that number exactly? The number of women who didn't know what to do with it? Because I assume the number of women who did know what to do with it is much larger than the women who didn't know what to do with it. So the number of women who didn't know what they were doing with it can't be that large. Like as a statistical pool."

"Wow." His face is unreadable for a moment as he

just stares at me. "So jealous," he says slowly then starts laughing again.

"So where does your cousin live?" I ask to deflect my odd possessive moment. Also because I'm wondering how often he visits his cousin and if he might want to visit me too. What? I'm a thinker. And O'Hare is a major hub. I could meet him at the airport for a quick layover. At the Hilton.

"He grew up in Connecticut," he begins and I almost groan out loud. I cannot catch a break. There cannot possibly be one flight pattern from London to Connecticut that routes through O'Hare. Not even the shitty cheap flights with crap layovers. "But he's in Las Vegas now," he adds. "Living there, for work."

Praise Jesus.

"Do you visit often?" In my head I imagine I'm asking this super-casually, but Jennings smirks with a brow raised and I'm pretty sure he's calling my bluff on this one.

"You're a big fan of Vegas, are you? Big gambler? Blackjack? Poker? Roulette, maybe?"

"I've never actually been." I pull my hand out from under his and pick nonchalantly at a piece of lint on my dress. "But I imagine myself to be fantastic at the slot machines."

"You're good at pushing buttons, that's for certain."

I flick my eyes back to his and place my hand on his leg again. Higher this time. I'm sitting near sideways on the seat so I can look at him while we talk and it gives me the leverage to slide my calf over his. Lightly. I inch my hand a bit higher and keep my eyes on his while holding his gaze for three seconds and smiling, because if it worked in a bar it most surely works in a backseat. I'm not entirely sure what I'm trying to accomplish though since I'd bet real Vegas money that I'm not going to bed alone tonight and I'm way too old to go at it in a backseat with someone else driving the car, even if I'm pretending to be someone I'm not this week. A girl has her limits.

Jennings tips his head closer to mine and covers my lips with his own, one hand on the nape of my neck to hold me steady as his lips brush over mine. Softly. But his other hand drags the hand I've placed mid-thigh up to the juncture of his legs. He squeezes my hand underneath his, forcing me to feel him through the denim barrier separating us.

I whimper, a silly little mumble from the back of my throat, and he smiles into the kiss, his lips curving against mine before he breaks us apart and touches his forehead to mine.

"Later," he promises with a wicked grin and one softly spoken word. Then he's opening the car door because the car has stopped and we've arrived. I blow out a breath to calm myself because he's just managed to work me up in the space of a nanosecond while I was attempting to seduce him. He threw that in my face, so to speak, didn't he?

My door opens and Jennings is waiting with a hand extended to assist me. Such a gentleman. A filthy, dirty gentleman.

CHAPTER TWENTY

Jennings

"Where are we?" She's exited the car and slipped her hand in mine, glancing at the building in front of us. She managed to miss the vineyard completely on the drive in, so focused on her task of seducing me.

She's an enigma, this girl. So full of passion but so innocently naïve about getting it. A mixture of sweet and sassy that makes me hard in an instant. The way her thoughts constantly play out across her face makes her easy to read but somehow all the more captivating. I can't get enough of her. How she tosses me a glare and rolls her eyes in my face when I've irked her. The way she bites her bottom lip and glances away while she thinks about how much she's willing to tell me. How her nose wrinkles and eyes narrow when I've crossed a line and how her pupils dilate when I've whispered something unexpectedly filthy in her ear.

Jesus, the smell of her alone is enough to get me going. The softness of her skin and the silk of her hair. The curve of her bottom and the swell of her tits.

I'm fucked.

"Local vineyard," I tell her. "They've a French restaurant that's rumored to be lovely."

She glances around, turning in a little circle to take in the property. We've been dropped at the entrance to the onsite inn, a charming building that looks like a house tucked away in the countryside. The vineyard stretches out in front of us, row after row of trellises covered in growing grape vines dotted by a perimeter of trees and open skies.

"Wow, you really go all out for first dates," Daisy says after she's completed her circle and returned to face me. "I'm impressed," she says and I wonder what her face would look like if I brought her to a French vineyard. Or a Spanish one. Or, best yet, a remote Italian vineyard in the countryside with a pool and staff who left during the day. We'd do nothing but eat and fuck and lie naked in the sun. I'd dribble the finest vintages money can buy across her skin and lap them up with my tongue a drop at a time.

"Don't get presumptuous about how good this date is. I could still ask you to split the bill," I deadpan.

She throws her head back and laughs and I can't recall the last time I enjoyed myself this much with anyone.

"I've never eaten French food before," she admits once we're inside sat at a table. Her fingertips are tapping the side of the menu and there's a small crease marring her forehead as she studies the options.

"No? If you don't enjoy it we'll stop at I Jump on the way back."

Her eyes fly up from the menu and she grins. "You're an excellent listener, Jennings."

"I'm a fast learner too. I already know three different ways to make you come in under ten minutes."

"Oh, my God." Her eyes widen and a blush covers her cheeks and I wonder if I can run an international travel business from Naperville, Illinois. Or, fuck it, perhaps I can retire at thirty-six and make my life's work finding the rest of the ways to make Daisy come.

What in the hell did my life look like before this woman? It's hard to recall.

The waiter collects our drink orders. I order a Manhattan while Daisy selects one of the Rieslings made at the on-site winery. She examines the interior of the restaurant, her eyes resting briefly on the wooden-beamed ceiling, chairs covered in a blue French toile fabric, and chandeliers hanging with their cords swagged from hooks in the ceiling. She doesn't speak until the drinks arrive.

She takes a sip of her wine and her eyes widen with pleasure. "Wow. That tastes like I could just suck it down."

Bloody hell.

She did not just say that. I grunt and shake my head to clear the memory of her on her knees sucking *me* down.

"Do you eat at restaurants like this often?" She asks it casually but that face of hers has already given her away, the question hanging in her eyes as she takes a sip of her drink.

"Occasionally," I tell her. Way to elaborate, Jennings.

She examines the tablecloth in front of her while I wait. They're royal blue, matching the blue print on the chairs.

"What is it you do exactly?"

There it is. The question I knew she wanted to ask. I should just tell her. Right now. Yet... something is holding me back. I've gotten in too deep on this lie of omission and now doesn't feel like the moment to correct it. Plus I need to figure her out before I lay out all my cards. There's something she's not telling me and I don't think the revelation that I'm her boss' boss' boss is going to get her to open up any. Likely the opposite. In fact I think it would have her hoofing it out the door.

"I work in operations for a London-based company."

"What does that mean?" She stares at me from across the table, her expression curious and relaxed.

Damn her curiosity.

"It's mostly analyzing strategies and procedures. Ensuring efficiencies. Minimizing resources. Forecasting trends, etcetera etcetera." I spout off a bunch of nonsense and hope it was dull enough to answer her and put an end to any additional questions.

"Wait a minute." She says the words slowly, her eyes narrowing. "I think I've got you figured out."

Shit. "Have you?" I take a sip of my drink and feign nonchalance.

"Yup. Can't fool me." She taps her water glass against the tablecloth as she speaks and I wonder if she's going to fling it in my face.

At least her hand isn't on the butter knife. Yet.

Fuck, I should have said something sooner. But it's not as though I lied, is it? An omission isn't a lie, exactly. I make a mental note not to say that aloud. I doubt it'll win me any points.

"You," she says, pointing at me with her finger and a stern expression, "have a job."

"Correct. And I don't live with my mum. We established that when you agreed to keep sleeping with me." I wink, hoping we're done with this line of conversation.

"I meant you have a good job." She tilts her head and examines me as if something is just occurring to her. "And you own a home. Even homes in the dodgy section of London are crazy expensive."

"Dodgy?" I laugh at her. Her expression is so serious, as if she's about to win a game of Clue. "Americans don't use the word 'dodgy' to describe property."

"I told you, I have an Anglophile fetish. Stop trying to

distract me." She straightens her silverware and I keep an eye on the knife. "I don't think your grandmother paid for your trip."

"No?"

"No. I think you paid for her trip. Am I right?" She sits back in her chair, confident she's solved the puzzle of me. "You let me think you were Mr. Good Times, but you have your act together, don't you?"

Not that together, no. But I grin and tell her it's family tradition to take turns taking Nan on holiday. Then the waiter arrives with our starters and I thank my lucky stars for the interruption.

I'm on borrowed time on this lie. I manage to remain relatively anonymous, being that no one gives a toss about who runs a travel conglomerate and I have a last name other than Sutton, but it's not impossible to piece together.

The company website is little more than a fancy landing site to direct consumers to the individual brands. The About section on the site only makes a brief mention of the corporation being family-owned, and even then not a name is listed, merely a note of four generations of service. She knows it surely, being an employee, but it's not my name on her payslip. I'm buried layers deeper than a contract employee of one division would care about.

I need to come clean with her.

"I think I've got you figured out as well." We've gotten a cheese board starter and Daisy pauses in the act of spreading raspberry preserve across a tiny crunchy toast and blinks twice.

"You have?"

"I think…" I pause, letting the tension build a moment while a look of unease flashes in her eyes. "I think that you like me."

She sets the toast on her bread plate and leans in a few inches before speaking.

"I think I'm addicted to having sex with you," she whispers and there's not an iota of seduction in her delivery. She presents it as if it's simply a fact that confuses her a bit. "It's really good, right? I'm sure I have less experience than you do, so maybe I'm just naïve. Or maybe I need a bigger sample pool? Maybe it's you and you're really good at sex and it's like this for you with everyone? Is it all the same to you? Maybe you're the common denominator?"

Totally guileless, this girl. She didn't say any of that from a place of judgement. It's from a place of curiosity and it's both endearing and erotic and oh, so totally Daisy.

"How am I supposed to eat this?" she asks, pointing at the cheese board. "I don't know what I'm doing."

"Spread the soft cheese onto the toast and eat it with your hands."

She does as I tell her and pops the food into her mouth, humming a little as the flavor hits her tongue. My cock responds as if she's just placed me on her tongue.

"This is fun," she says, doing a little wiggle in her seat. "You're fun, Jennings."

Fun? When's the last time someone accused me of being fun?

"So is it always good for you? The sex, I mean. Not the cheese. Cheese is always good, am I right? There's nothing not to enjoy about a liaison with cheese. In your mouth." She's babbling and she makes a grab for her wine glass before adding, "Yay, cheese." Then she downs a long sip and avoids my eyes.

Jesus Christ, she has no game.

I rub a hand over my jaw and think about my response. I need to tread carefully because this is a conversation that could result in me heading to my room alone tonight before I know what's hit me. The last thing I need her thinking about is any woman who isn't her.

"Daisy," I say softly and wait for her eyes to return to mine. "You're the most fun I've ever had."

She dips her head and smiles, a blush coloring her face over the double entendre. "I'm not that experienced in fun."

"Why is that?" I ask when what I want to say is, *Good.*

She shrugs and works on preparing another toast. "Focused on my career. Wasted time on the wrong guys. You know, the usual reasons."

"Tell me about the guy."

"Which one?"

"The one who led you to pick up a stranger in a hotel bar." *The idiot who led you straight to me.*

She wiggles her nose while she thinks about what, if anything, she wants to share and I focus on not asking for the cheque and dragging her out of here caveman-style so I can fuck the answers out of her.

"It's sorta tied into my old job."

Fucking hell. I don't think I like where this is headed.

"The design job? That you did prior to working at Sutton Travel?"

"Right." She fidgets in her seat. "A long time ago."

I wonder what a long time consists of in a twenty-six-year-old's life.

"So what happened?" I prompt.

"It's embarrassing," she says while examining the crumbs on her plate.

"How so? You were co-workers? Dating the boss?" Fuck, neither of these options are great. No wonder she was squirrelly about company policies.

"We were co-workers, yes." She pauses. "And his dad owned the company."

Fuck.

"I sound like a hussy when I say that, right? I promise you I did not get any special treatment. None!" Her eyes flash with an old pain and I wish I could erase it for her. "It wasn't like that at all. At all," she repeats.

"Of course you didn't."

"It was the opposite of an advantage. I didn't push hard enough to get the projects I wanted because I didn't want anyone to think I got them unfairly."

"I get it," I tell her, and I do. I get the conflict, if not the holding back. Working at a family-owned business, you know you're being watched more than anyone else. You know you have to work twice as hard to prove yourself worthy of the advancements that you've earned, but were always expected to receive.

"Then the company was sold and most of the staff was laid off, myself included. Mark relocated with the new company so I lost my job, my boyfriend and my house in the same week."

"You were living together?" I hate the idea of this.

"No." She shakes her head. "No. I was in the process of buying a condo and it fell through when I got laid off. Banks frown upon a lack of employment."

Bloody arsehole.

"Never again, you know? I never should have gone out with him. What's that saying? 'Don't mix business and pleasure?' Yeah, don't."

"I prefer the saying 'never say never.'"

"You do? Why?"

Because you're involved with a co-worker right now and you don't know it yet. Because I can't envision walking away from you when this week is over and I need you to forgive me for not telling you sooner.

The waiter arrives with our entrées and I take the opportunity to avoid the question. When he leaves Daisy continues.

"If my work and personal life hadn't been combined it wouldn't have all blown up at once," she says.

"Sometimes a shake-up is just what you need," I counter.

She frowns at me when I say that and I realize I might be overdoing it.

"Did you consider going with him?" Hell, there I go again. Asking her questions out of context. Because what I mean is, *Is Naperville fucking Illinois a hard limit for you?*

She blinks a few times and pokes at her food. "I don't know," she finally says. "Because he didn't ask. Looking back I'd like to say no, I wouldn't have. Knowing everything I know now, I'd like to say no way. But I don't really know, do I? He hadn't shared any of his plans with me," she continues. "I didn't expect that he'd disclose the company was being sold. I honestly didn't. But he could have found a way to tell me something. He could have told me he was considering a move. That he'd been recruited to another company. He could have told me that much, but he didn't. The weekend I thought he was on a golf trip with friends he was in California signing a lease on a new apartment. He was full of lies and half-truths."

"He's obviously an idiot. Terrible in bed as well, I suspect."

She grins, the smile lighting up her face and the hint of sadness in her eyes gone.

"Nowhere near as fun as you," she says. Then she laughs, delighted in her dirty pun, and I add this look on her face to all the others I can't get enough of.

CHAPTER TWENTY-ONE

Jennings

"So what about you?" Daisy asks. "I showed you mine, now you show me yours. Tell me something embarrassing."

"I don't think that's quite how that game is played, love, but if you want to play kinky show and tell later I'm up for it." Literally. "You didn't tell me anything embarrassing. You told me about a wanker you used to date. An embarrassing story would be something like getting caught skinny-dipping as a teenager or walking into the wrong bathroom in primary school."

"Did you do those things?" Her eyes are wide and she's leaned forward a bit, eager to hear my stories of youthful mortification.

"Possibly."

"Tell me," she says, leaning back in her chair again. She's ordered the risotto and as she places a forkful in her mouth her shoulders drop and she closes her eyes in apparent happiness. When she opens them she raises her brow to prompt me to get on with my confessions.

"I'll go first. Given you've not had a turn." I level her a look of mock seriousness. "And because I'm a gentleman." I stab my fork into a vegetable on my plate as I think up something suitably embarrassing to share. "Once in primary school I accidentally called a teacher Mum. I was teased mercilessly for the rest of the school term."

"In third grade I threw up on the bus. Directly onto the boy I had my first crush on. He never spoke to me again."

"In secondary school I said the word 'orgasm' instead of 'organism' whilst giving a presentation in class."

"I accidentally texted 'I love you' to my camp counselor instead of my mom."

"I got caught skinny-dipping with Melissa Peterson. In the school pool. By her father, the headmaster."

She stares at me, her lips pursed to the side and her fingers tapping the tablecloth. I think she's trying to come up with something more embarrassing, so I wait patiently.

"When I was a kid, I'd get out of the bathtub and streak through the house yelling 'cold naked kid' while my mom attempted to catch me with a towel."

"You did not."

"I did. I promise you I did."

"It hardly counts, you were a toddler."

"I didn't stop until the second grade."

We stare at each other in silence before we both burst into laughter.

"I have no idea what I was thinking," she says, still giggling. "But it seemed a really necessary part of bathing at the time."

"I'll take you to a topless beach if you're so eager."

"No! No way! Never."

"You've grown out of your exhibitionist stage, then?"

"Yes. Most definitely."

"Tell me something more recent. Perhaps an embarrassing university story."

"Freshman year," she says without missing a beat. She grabs her wine glass and takes a swig as if she needs the fortification for this story, and I'm already trying not to smile. "I almost dropped out of college over this, I was so mortified."

"Do tell." The most delightful blush has begun to warm her cheeks and I'm captivated with her.

"I've got an afternoon class across campus. I'm not in a rush because I was that nerd who arrived ten minutes early for everything and sat in the front row." She shakes her head and rolls her eyes at herself and I immediately imagine a prim and proper college-aged Daisy wearing glasses and saucy pony tail. I like this image very much. "And we've gotten a frost so I've allotted extra time on top of my extra time."

"You took nerding seriously."

"Very." She nods in agreement. "So I exit my dorm, middle of the day. Kids are everywhere." She waves a hand in front of her in an arc to indicate the totality of everywhere. "I get ten feet outside my dorm and decide to cut across the grass because I love that crunching sound that frozen grass makes when you walk on it." She closes her eyes and sighs, then shakes her head slightly to fortify herself before opening her eyes to continue. "Then I wiped out. Bam. On my ass. In front of a billion kids." She shakes her head again. "I know, I know. Before you say anything, I know people fall all the time, blah blah." She exhales and takes another sip of her wine. "But there's more."

"Okay." I grin, loving the way she can't even look at me right now.

"When I go down, I hear a rip."

I laugh and then she does look at me.

"It gets worse. This super-cute guy from my dorm stops to help me up, but I don't want his help because I suspect my ass is hanging out of my pants, you know? So I try to wave him off but he thinks I'm offering him a hand to give me a boost to my feet. Once I'm up I grab my butt to determine how bad the damage is and I think I'm playing it off as if I'm just wiping the seat of my pants off, but he thinks I'm hurt so he asks if I'm okay and somehow this ends with him looking at my ass. Literally, because this was freshman year, when I decided to assert my newfound independence by wearing thong panties."

"That's pretty bad," I agree with a sympathetic nod.

"I couldn't make eye contact with that guy for the rest of the semester."

"But did you make it to class on time?" I attempt to ask this with a straight face but fail.

"Ha ha," she snaps and glances quickly away, but a moment later she mumbles, "Yes."

"You went to class after that? You really were a nerd."

"Yeah. The very worst part is that I was wearing sensible boots. My sensible boots did not save me from falling on my ass."

"Bit of a disaster, weren't you?"

"Yup."

"Did you get laid at all in university?"

"Not till junior year."

I laugh out loud then. This girl.

"I'm still traumatized by the sound of ripping denim."

"I'd imagine so, love. I'd imagine so."

CHAPTER TWENTY–TWO

Violet

The sexual tension in the backseat of the car on the way back to the hotel is off the charts. At least, it is to me, but there's no way he's not feeling it too. It's like a tangible line strumming between us. His arm is wrapped around my shoulder, fingertip lightly stroking the outer curve of my breast. My hand is on his thigh, leisurely caressing up and down. Quiet kisses leave no doubt how tonight ends.

The car—a car service, not an Uber, I learned when the same SUV was waiting for us after dinner—drops us at the front door of the hotel. Jennings takes my hand and we walk inside, the motion-activated doors whooshing behind us. We're quiet as we head to the elevators, hands entwined, and I imagine we look like a couple who's content with one another instead of one who's only just met. I feel comfortable with him.

When we reach the door to my room he stops and turns me to face him, leaning down and kissing me. His lips press softly against mine, one hand behind my neck and the other resting on my hip. He nips my bottom lip between his teeth before breaking the kiss and taking a half step back, running his hand across his jaw and lower lip. "Good night," he says, a heated spark in his eyes. Then he turns around and starts walking back to the elevators.

What. The hell?

"Where are you going?" I whisper-yell it at his retreating figure, because it is late and this is a family-friendly hotel.

He stops, turns, but doesn't walk back. There's three or four feet separating us when we should be naked with nothing between us besides a thin layer of latex covering his cock.

"My room." He points a thumb over his shoulder toward the elevators. "First date. I've escorted you to your door and kissed you good night accordingly."

"Are you freaking kidding me?" I'm pretty sure my jaw is on the floor.

"No?" He raises one brow in challenge. "I assumed coming in was off the table on a first date. I seem to recall you mentioning it in your litany of first-date rules."

"For normal guys. You're not normal."

"So I'm special? Or odd?" He rolls his bottom lip between his teeth and cocks his head to the side. I don't miss the grin that sneaks across his face either.

"Are you trying to make me beg? Besides, they were guidelines, not rules," I add as I stand taller and lift my chin in defiance, arms crossed over my chest.

"Ah, guidelines. So they're optional then?"

"They're guidelines. You know, to guide. Like a suggestion, not a law."

"Ahh. I see." He nods but he's still not moving. "I do rather like the idea of you begging, love. Now that you've mentioned it." He takes one step towards me and stops. "Invite me in, then."

He really is making me work for this.

"Would you like to come inside?" The words come out softer than I intended, more seductive, and I blush at the double meaning and tap the keycard in my hand against my forehead with a tiny groan.

Jennings grins, studying me with mirth-filled eyes, then steps forward and takes the key from my hand.

"Undress," he commands the moment the door clicks shut behind us.

"Just like that?"

"I can do it for you if you'd rather."

"Okay." I shrug. "You do it."

He pauses, appearing caught off guard for a moment, and then a slow smile covers his face. He stops in the midst of unbuttoning his shirt and meets my eyes. I think he's stealing my three-second eye-contact trick and being on the receiving end, let me tell you, it's very, very effective. My breath is caught in my throat and I feel on the verge of trembling when he closes the short distance between us and stops. He runs a single fingertip across my collarbone and I feel it—everywhere. My pulse races, my nipples harden and I'm so wet he could take me right now with ease.

"You continually surprise me, love."

"Do I?"

"Indeed." His lips replace his fingertip and I shudder. Then he moves to my earlobe and nips the shell with his teeth before removing my earrings, first from one ear then the other. How that's erotic is beyond me but the gentle touch of his fingertips as he slides the loops free from my ears is having an effect.

"I like it." I pause for a moment, unsure of saying this out loud. "I like it when you take charge. When you're a little bossy." Heat floods my core just hearing myself say it and I fidget both for relief and out of awkwardness. Is it weird to admit that?

"I know," he replies with amusement in his tone and my gaze snaps to his. He winks.

Holy crap, that does things to me.

"Would it be embarrassing if I came before my clothes are off?" Because it's a real possibility.

"Not for you, no. It'd be embarrassing if I came before your clothes were off, though, wouldn't it?"

"Yeah. Sorry about that, by the way."

"About?" he questions as his hand skims the hemline of my dress, his fingertips stroking the outside of my thigh.

"Sorry that you can only come once while I get to come multiple times. It's hardly fair, is it? I never realized that it was possible. I mean, I knew it was possible for some women, like porn stars and sexual-type people who are gifted or just lucky, but I didn't know it was possible for me." *Oh, my God, stop talking.*

I can't see his face but I hear his soft laugh in my ear, his breath warm against my neck. "Happy to provide an education, love." He kisses the spot where my neck meets my shoulder and I shiver. "Turn around."

I turn, my eyes on the window. The sheer curtain is covering the window for privacy but the blackout curtain is still open, allowing the parking lot lights to filter into the room.

The zipper of my dress is making the slowest progression down my back in the history of zippers. Inch by lackadaisical inch. I'm hyper-aware of him standing behind me, the descent of the zipper and the heat of his body driving me slowly insane.

Then he's slipping the material from my shoulders, the fabric sliding down my arms and over my hips. Jennings crouches behind me with the material around my ankles and instructs me to step out before he rises with the dress in hand. It makes a barely audible whisper of a sound as it lands on the dresser and then he's back, gathering my hair and sweeping it over one shoulder and caressing the other with his lips.

The clasp of my bra gives way beneath his fingers and is quickly discarded on top of my dress, his lips never leaving my neck. His chest presses to my back as he pinches my nipple. I gasp, my head falling forward to watch his hand cupping my breast and twisting the nipple between finger and thumb. His other hand is splayed across my lower stomach, holding me to him. The buttons from his shirt press into my back and I grind my ass against him, reassured to feel that he's as affected as I am.

Then his hand dips into the front of my panties and I moan. I wasn't expecting it and the mere skimming of his fingers over my skin has me saying a silent prayer he'll give me the relief I'm aching for.

"I adore how wet you are for me," he murmurs into my ear while his fingers slide through my slit, dragging the moisture to my clit.

It feels a little obscene, watching his hand dip into my underwear. Dirtier, somehow, than if I was simply naked. I can't take my eyes off the sight, his thumb visible above the waistband while his fingers delve below.

I grind my bottom harder against his erection and am rewarded with him increasing the pressure with his hand, pulling me tighter to hold me still. The result is more friction exactly where I need it and I buck my hips against his hand with the limited amount of movement available to me because I still want more. More pressure. More contact. More Jennings.

His cock is rock hard against my bottom. I imagine it straining against his pants, eager to be inside of me, and I emit something resembling a groan. I'm so close to release.

He slips two fingers inside of me and I bite my lip. So close.

"You're awfully assertive for a woman who just told me she likes to defer control."

I grin, knowing he can't see it. "I know, it's just that I'm so fond of your hand."

"I can tell. You're riding it so shamelessly my cock is getting jealous." He pinches my nipple again and I clench around his fingers. "You're soaking my hand, love. I'll have to suck my fingers clean when you're done."

"Jennings." I exhale his name in a rush. My thighs tense and the pressure builds to the point I don't think I can take any more. I feel so uninhibited with him, like the only thing that matters is enjoying each other, and it's the most incredible turn-on I've ever experienced.

I've still got my head tilted down, watching the motion of his hand as he works me. Watching as his thumb slips under the waistband of my panties and presses against my clit, as he curves his fingers inside of me and nips my earlobe with his teeth, and I shatter.

I'd be on the ground if I wasn't pressed so firmly against him because my legs are useless. A strong arm wrapped around my ribcage keeps me from going down as his other hand pushes me to ride the orgasm longer than I knew was possible.

When the wave subsides, I test putting weight on my legs before stumbling, a little orgasm-drunk, from his grip as I turn to face him.

"Holy crap, how are you still fully clothed?" I blink at him, trying to recall how we got here. "Like how is it possible that I just came that hard when only one of us is naked?"

"You can take off the knickers now." His eyes are on mine as he unbuttons his shirt, his movements steady and unhurried.

That's right. I'm not even completely naked. I hook my thumbs into the material and slide them over my hips until they hit the floor.

"Hand them to me," he instructs.

I grab them from the floor and feel my face flush as I hand them to him, which is ridiculous after what he just did to me. Yet it's still sort of mortifying to hand him a pair of panties that he just helped me make extremely damp.

"Lie on the bed," he instructs as the last button from his shirt is freed. I do so, keeping my eyes on his hands as they move to his belt. What is it about watching a man unbuckle his belt that is so freaking arousing?

"Face down."

That I wasn't expecting. I blink at him for a moment, watching the leather slip free of the buckle, and then slowly roll over with my arms bent and tucked to my sides.

"Ass up."

Oh, holy fuck. Okay. I wonder if my ass is blushing as much as my face is. Is that a thing? I'm so stimulated right now I feel as though I must be flushed everywhere. I slide my knees up and push myself onto my elbows so that my ass will be higher than my head, thinking that's what he wants based on the limited instructions.

Then I wait.

I hear his pants come off, the belt buckle making an iota of a sound as it hits the floor, but enough for me to guess where he's at in his disrobing process. Then his hands are on my hips and I'm sliding across the sheets until my knees and ass are at the edge of the bed.

Then the tip of his cock is nudging my entrance. I fist the sheets with my hands as he slams into me with one solid stroke. He grunts. I groan and dip my head, focusing on steadying my forearms against the bed so I don't end up on my face.

Jennings grips my hips, his fingers digging into my flesh as he pounds into me. The room is silent apart from the sound of skin slapping against skin and labored breathing. I'm a vessel for his pleasure and I love it. My tits are bouncing with the force of his thrusts and his balls are hitting my clit. He's so damn deep like this and the angle is bliss.

I need to see what he looks like right now.

I need to see the expression on his face that accompanies the grunts leaving his mouth. The look in his eyes as he's whispering filthy things about the view of my ass. The clench of his jaw as he flexes his hips and pounds into me. I need a snapshot in my mind of what he looks like to remember this by.

I look over my shoulder, my hair sweeping across my back and half covering my face, but it's enough for a glimpse.

His eyes burn into mine, hooded and intent. His lips are slightly parted and his tongue swipes his bottom lip as I watch. It immediately makes me think of his tongue on my clit and I clench around his cock, shocked I'm this close to coming again. I turn back with a moan, dipping my forehead to the mattress, arching my back and pushing my ass higher up.

It doesn't last long though because a second later Jennings yanks my hair and pulls me into a kneeling position in front of him with his lips against my neck.

The words, "Did you want to watch, love?" are not even out of his mouth before I'm coming hard on his cock.

It's too much, too much stimulation too quickly. I

might fall apart from the pleasure and I don't think I can take it, but Jennings holds me against him and stills as my pussy clenches painfully tight around him. I drop my head onto his shoulder and try to push him away because it's too much; I'm ultra-sensitive and in an orgasmic free fall.

As I come down Jennings slips out of me and places his palm over my pussy with soothing hushed words in my ear, telling me how beautiful I am and how amazed he is with me. His hand cups me intimately, but not erotically. He's not thumbing my clit or fingering me. His dick is still hard and pressed against my ass between us and his hand cups me, the sensation warm and soothing and loving.

He settles me onto the bed, on my back now, and braces himself on top of me, his arms pressed to the mattress on either side of my head to keep from crushing me. His cock slides back into me like it was always meant to be there.

Slow strokes, deep and measured. I wrap my arms around his neck and bend one knee, my ankle resting on his ass. Our lips meet, matching the pace of our sex, deliberate yet soft. My heart is racing but it's so much more than adrenaline.

"Is this real?" I whisper it, meant more for myself than him, but his eyes answer my question; his gaze moves across my face with tenderness before a, "Yes," is pressed onto my lips. I pull him closer so I can bury my face in his neck, my nipples pressed against his chest. He smells like sex and soap and maybe a hint of clove or nutmeg— something I can't put my finger on but is uniquely Jennings.

The weight of his cock when he slides into me is pure rapture, heavy and thick. Each penetration fills me with warmth and fullness, each retreat met by a buck of my hips begging for his return. The intensity escalates with each thrust but in a quiet way, the frenzied pace of earlier abandoned, replaced with a different sort of passion. Tender and affectionate. Nothing else matters but the two of us, right here, right now.

"This is a really great date," I say softly.

"The best ever," he agrees, his forehead touching mine. I run a hand over his jaw and he presses a kiss into my palm before pushing back onto his arms and adjusting the leg I have wrapped around him. He hooks my knee over his elbow and thrusts deep, the penetration making me cry out his name as I come again. His cock pulses as he joins me, thrusting twice more before stilling inside of me.

He rolls us so I'm lying atop him, still inside of me as our heart rates slow.

"I can't move," I tell him, even though I'm the one on top. I'm not making an effort to be light, splayed on top of him, my limbs limp noodles and my head using his chest as a pillow.

If I've ever been this satiated before in my entire life I can't recall it.

Jennings cups the back of my head and rolls me onto my back, kissing my forehead before he rises. I grunt at the upheaval and whine about the loss of his body heat.

"Don't move," he says.

"I just said I'm incapable, you sex maniac." I flop my hand halfheartedly onto the mattress. "I might never recover. I'll probably get fired tomorrow because I'll be unable to move. I'll point to the attractions as we pass them and say, 'Sorry, folks, we can't get off the bus because I'm unable to walk due to the sex marathon I had last night.' That should go over well."

"You won't get sacked," he calls out on his way into the bathroom. Holy crap, he has a really nice ass. How has that escaped my attention? I think I might be an ass girl. Wait. That didn't sound right even in my head. His ass, not mine. Nope, still not right.

"You don't know that. I could still fuck this trip up." *You have no idea how true this is.*

"I'll put in a good word for you." His voice echoes a bit from the bathroom. The door is open and the water is running but I can't see him from where I'm at.

"How? You're the one causing the disruption. I hardly think you'd get a vote." Men, Jesus. They think they can solve anything.

The water stops and Jennings steps from the bathroom. The view is good from this side too, so help me. It makes my breath catch in my throat to look directly at him. He's such a man—I know that sounds dumb, of course he's a man. But like, holy shit, he's a *man*. Tall, filled out. Sculpted abs and a strong jaw. His veins are hot, for crying out loud. The ones on the backs of his hands drive me wild with distraction. The way they trail up his arms, perfection. And the one large one running the length of his dick? I'm a big fan of that one. Big, big fan.

As he steps closer to the bed I notice he's got a washcloth in his hand. Hold up. Is he?

He is.

"Oh, my God." I slap my hands over my face and attempt to snap my knees together as he lowers the cloth to my bare pussy. It's warm and wet—and oh, Jesus, so am I—and this is really, really embarrassing. Jennings doesn't seems to have any qualms about cleaning me up though, pressing my knee outward with his other hand to widen my legs as I squeak beneath my hands.

"You said you were too tired to get up."

"This is so dirty."

"This is dirty?" There's laughter in his voice. "You coming all over my hand was dirty. Your ass bent over the bed was dirty. Shagging you until you're too tired to walk was dirty. This isn't dirty. This is revering your pussy."

I peek at him between my fingers. "Revering? Really?"

The pressure of his hand through the washcloth increases. He drags it across the inside of one thigh then the other. My skin tingles in its wake as he dips to my core and finishes his task. I'm turned on again and more than a little flustered. No one has ever done more than hand me a paper towel before.

"Like a religious experience, love."

"With my pussy?"

"I hold your pussy in the highest of esteem," he says with a straight face.

I groan and he laughs.

This guy is so much trouble.

CHAPTER TWENTY-THREE

Violet

The next two days fly by in a blur. I'm floating on the high of the best date—and the best sex—I've ever had. There's a spring in my step, a smile on my face and hope in my bruised heart.

I'm nailing the tour guide gig thing and nailing Jennings at the same time. In fact, I think I'm going to update my résumé and add multitasking under my useful skills.

In Williamsburg, while the group happily watches blacksmiths forge iron into tools the same way they would have during days gone by, Jennings pulls me around the corner and kisses me until I'm breathless.

In Jamestown, as the group takes a tour of a recreation of the three ships that brought America's first English colonists to Virginia in 1607, Jennings drags me into an alcove past the ticket office, slips one hand under my skirt and makes me come, his other hand clamped firmly over my mouth the moment before I would have given us away.

In Richmond—oh, Richmond. Our stop in Richmond is to visit St. John's Church, the spot where the American Revolution was ignited when Patrick Henry made the famous "Give me liberty or give me death" speech. While the group enjoys a guided tour of the church and sits in the original pews—pews George Washington and Thomas Jefferson themselves might well have sat in— Jennings and I are in the bathroom having sex.

I'm not sure I'll ever be able to think of Richmond without blushing.

We drive through the Shenandoah National Park and the Blue Ridge Mountains on our way to Gettysburg. The views are spectacular and the time spent sitting next to Jennings chatting about nothing and everything is—well, it is everything.

At one stop we find an arcade and I kick his butt in ski-ball. At another he takes me to dinner at an IHOP and I torture him by moaning as I stuff pancakes into my mouth, his eyes darkening as I try not to laugh with my mouth full.

We exchange stories from childhood, mine carefully edited not to include any mention of Daisy. I ask him questions about living in London and make him recite words I find especially attractive in his accent.

He asks me about my goals. I've never been with a man so interested in what I want out of my future. He even offered to look over my résumé—he mentioned he does some of the hiring at his company and would be happy to look over my résumé and give me some pointers. Only he called it a CV, so I'd no idea what he was referring to at first. Based on the conversation we were having at the time I sorta got that he wasn't offering me a sexual favor, but it still took me a moment to catch on.

I deferred the offer, obviously. Even if I could have quickly changed my name to Daisy's, I'd have had to add Sutton Travel on there somewhere and I've been avoiding any concrete answers about how long I've been doing this tour guide gig.

The point is that he cared enough to offer.

But still, I haven't told him. That my name is Violet, not Daisy. I hardly remember it most of the time, the lie. I feel more myself with him than I've felt in a long, long time.

Somehow I've managed to justify it in my own head. It's not even that odd to me that the guests all call me Daisy. I've heard the name my entire life. I've been called Daisy accidentally more times than I can count. In school, with friends, by my own parents. It's second nature to respond to it as if it were my own name. The only person who really matters is Jennings, and most of the time he calls me 'love.' In front of the other guests he calls me Daisy. Or Miss Hayden. But when it's just us it's 'love.' And I convince myself that it's a small technicality—as if my actual real name is insignificant. It's me he's spending time with, not Daisy.

I'll tell him after—if there is an after. We haven't talked about the future—not in specific detail, anyway. I've told him about my background in design, keeping it as vague as possible. I've mentioned that I'm looking for another job in that field and he's questioned if I'm willing to relocate for work. Relocate to London? I'm not entirely sure that's what he was asking. Perhaps he was asking if I'd move to New York or Los Angeles or Detroit if the right job came along.

But he did ask it.

He did mention a meeting he has in New York in a couple of months. And his cousin in Las Vegas. Were those invitations? Feelers?

And he suggested that I could look for a position at the parent company of Sutton Travel—which is located in London. He mentioned it twice, in fact. Reminded me about what an Anglophile I am—and I don't think I was imagining the silent look he gave me when he said it, a whole conversation passing between us without words.

And...

I did it. I applied for a job in London. Two of them, in fact. I mean, fuck it, right? I've dreamed of living overseas my entire life. If now's not the time, when? Most everything I own was packed into a storage unit when I moved in with Daisy and honestly, I don't even miss my stuff, not really. It's just stuff. I could sell off most of it at this point and not think twice about it. Pack up a few suitcases and move anywhere. What do I need besides my laptop, cell and some personal items?

Jennings.

I need Jennings.

But it's not like I'd be moving just for him—it would be for me too. Because in the long run of my life, what's more important? Playing it safe or taking risks? Playing it safe hasn't gotten me what I expected. If anything, it's the safe choices I regret.

Both with my career and my heart.

So why the hell not reach for the stars? Do something crazy? Crazier than a one-night stand. Something with no sure outcome.

We'll see how things play out.

Until then, I'm on cloud nine.

Giddy about the possibilities. Optimistic about my career. Enchanted with Jennings.

It doesn't last long.

CHAPTER TWENTY-FOUR

Violet

The stop in Gettysburg went off without a hitch. We toured the battlefield where the Civil War ended and the site where Abraham Lincoln delivered the Gettysburg Address. In the afternoon the group took a walking tour with a local expert while I returned calls to my recruiter and sent off a few more résumés.

That evening we had another group dinner. They're included with the tour, and fun, even if they take forever. Jennings sat with his nan and eyed me at the table I shared with George and a couple from Canada, winking at me while no one was looking.

Afterwards we went to his room and watched a movie while we waited for dessert from room service. I have no idea how the movie ended, but I'm sure I'll catch the rest of it on cable sometime. Totally worth it.

Then—before I know what's hit me—we're en route to our final stop on this tour. The week I went into kicking and screaming I'm now wishing would last just a little bit longer. I'll miss this group. It's crazy how fast you can bond when you travel together. How quickly you develop inside jokes and find little quirks in people that endear them to you. I'll miss the way Mrs. Jarvis stops to take a photo of every interesting door we pass. How Mr. Boero cannot leave a stop without a souvenir magnet.

How Mrs. Delaine compares the coffee at every stop to Tim Hortons and how Isaac—a young man traveling by himself from Africa—insists on telling the group riddles while we travel from city to city. Except they never make any sense.

"A woman swims across a river of crocodiles to get to a party, but she doesn't die. Why?"

The punchline? Because she was at the party.

So. Stupid. Yet he made an impression and now I'll never see him again. I don't know how my sister does this. I'm a homebody. I get attached. I'm already sad about saying goodbye to this group when we haven't even parted yet.

**

Our final stop is Philadelphia, which makes me happy. I went to college here—at Penn—and I love any opportunity to visit my old stomping grounds. Just being back in the city is filling me with nostalgia. Now that I'm here, I'm kicking myself for not arranging a coffee date with my old school friends. I haven't seen the girls since Chloe's wedding, but I was so wrapped up in the anxiety of pulling off this tour guide gig I didn't think of it until now. Maybe I'll send a group text later, see who's available.

We're booked into a hotel downtown in the Society Hill area on a tree-lined street still paved with bricks—it's part of the charm I love in an old city. The Delaware river is a block away and my old dorm room is less than five miles from here, just on the other side of the Schuylkill. Thinking of it reminds me of all the hope I felt at graduation. The way the possibilities of the world felt endless and all I had to do was jump.

I lost that somewhere in the four years since.

I'm not losing it again.

My attempt to get my groove back with a sexy stranger turned into so much more than I expected. More than a kickstart. More than affirmation. It gave me my life back, in a sense—reminded me of the glee of the unknown. The sheer joy of a blank slate and endless options.

Today we're going on a walking tour of Philadelphia. It's the final day of the tour and we've got a local expert who will be leading the tour. All I have to do is trail behind and make sure no one gets lost. Tomorrow the coach will make two trips to the airport to drop the guests and then it's over. If I can get through today I've pulled this off. And today should be easy. I know Philly. Granted, I wasn't frequenting historic sites much during my university years, but I'm familiar enough with each of our stops today to answer anything I'd be expected to know about this city without Daisy's notebook.

I'm in the home stretch.

There's a bounce to my step as I arrive in the lobby to greet the group. An actual bounce. I pulled this off—well, almost. But today will be a piece of cake, so yeah, I've pulled it off.

Minus the one thing.

I haven't figured out how to tell Jennings my name is Violet yet.

Tiny detail, really.

I gnaw on my lip and wonder if he has to know. *Of course he has to know,* I chide myself. If this is going to continue—if we're going to continue—I have to tell him everything. As much as I feel like what's happened between us is real, only one of us has the facts.

I'll tell him after. The end of the trip is so close now it doesn't make sense to mention it today. Or tonight.

Tomorrow. I'll tell him tomorrow.

He'll probably think it's funny.

It's sorta funny. Right?

Fuck.

"Daisy!" Someone is calling my sister's name as I walk across the lobby. I can't place the voice and as I turn to follow it, I find a man in maybe his late thirties or early forties approaching me with a wide smile. He's very good-looking. I've never seen him before, but since he's calling me Daisy I'll assume Daisy has—and prepare myself to fake it until I can figure out if they know each other. I say a silent prayer that they don't 'know' each other.

He's wearing a polo with a logo of the walking tour we're taking today and holding a small white envelope that he extends in my direction.

"Hey." I smile at the guy. It appears his name is Gary, based on a name badge pinned to his shirt. I take the envelope from his hand. Daisy's name is handwritten on the front in large letters that appear to be the penmanship of a girl under ten. The pink glitter ink helps me narrow it down.

"Um, thank you," I offer. *Please, please fill me in on what this is about*, I think to myself as Jennings arrives in the lobby and stops beside us. I glance at the envelope and back to Gary again. "This is so nice." At least I think it is. Maybe this guy is a psycho who writes Daisy letters in childish handwriting. Why did she not clue me in on a potential Gary issue in Philadelphia? They've clearly worked together on this tour before; he definitely seems to know her. She never was one for formulating a solid plan though. 'Daisy's my pantser,' Mom always says. 'Violet's my planner.'

"From my daughter," Gary says, and I do my best not

to audibly sigh in relief. "Thank you so much for helping her set up her blog. She said she's up to three hundred followers. She's pretty excited." He laughs and shakes his head.

"Oh, that was so nice of—" I'm about to say 'her.' As in, *That was so nice of Daisy to help this kid.* Except I'm Daisy right now, so I'd be complimenting myself. "So nice of her to write a thank you note." I ad-lib that reply like a pro. That was close. Time to wrap this up before it goes bad.

"She loved your photography tips too."

"Photography tips," Jennings mutters to himself under his breath.

"She said the way you explained moving around the shot for variety and working from the back of a scene forward changed how she sets up a shot. Whatever that means." Gary laughs.

I laugh too, a fake ha-ha kind of laugh. "Yeah, those are my best tips."

"She's such a fan of your blog."

"You have a blog?" Jennings looks interested in that tidbit of information.

"Um, thank you!" I beam a smile at Gary and take a half step away in the direction of the group waiting in the lobby. "She's a sweetheart." I have no idea if this is true, but everyone thinks their kid is great, so I'm sure I can't go wrong with a compliment, factual or not.

"We should stay on schedule," I add, pointing a thumb towards the door. "Thank you for the thank you." I wave the card in the air and take another half step. "Give her my regards." My regards? She's a child. "I mean, tell her I said hi!" I quickly amend.

"Of course. Kaia adores you. She wanted to tag along again today but she had a traveling soccer game."

I say a silent prayer of thanks, because you know who's great at telling twins apart? Children. They're like little bullshit detectors.

"Soccer is important," I agree. I have no idea what I'm talking about. "So, ready to get this tour started?" I don't wait for a response, just spin on my heel and start walking towards the group waiting by the lobby doors.

I make it two steps before Jennings has questions.

"What's your blog about?"

"It's a travel blog."

"A travel blog," he repeats. "But I thought design was your passion."

"It is. I just do the travel blog for fun."

"Right," he says slowly, as if that doesn't make sense.

Rightfully so, because who does a thing they're not really that interested in for fun?

"Well, I'd love to see it," he says.

"Sure."

Hell, no. Like I need him asking me more questions I can't answer? I don't think so.

"I'll show you later," I lie. By then we've reached the group, so I do what any good liar does—I change the subject.

"Is everyone ready?" I turn my attention to the group and do a quick head count. "Looks like we're all here!" I chirp in false excitement. I'm not normally this chirpy. I need to tone it down because Jennings is looking at me strangely.

CHAPTER TWENTY-FIVE
Jennings

We exit the hotel, Daisy trailing the group to keep an eye out and make sure no one lags behind. I stuff my headset into my pocket and walk beside her, neither of us speaking. Daisy seems jittery and I'm not sure why.

We have to talk. Tonight. Tomorrow I fly to Connecticut to bring Nan to my aunt and then I'm on a flight back to London.

There's no way in hell I'm leaving without knowing when I'm going to see her again.

Or bringing her with me.

"So you enjoy photography?" I ask to break the silence. She shrugs and mumbles something about it helping her blog. How did I not know this about her? There are so many things I don't know about her.

Yet.

But I will.

Maybe it's cocky, but I know enough.

I know enough to know what we could be together.

We have a connection and sometimes the intangible force between two people is stronger than reason. Stronger than time and logic. Stronger than knowing things like what flavor crisps they like best. Or their favorite show. Or if they've got especially strong opinions on which way the loo roll hangs.

Wait—I do know one of those things. Barbecue crisps, she said. I know amusement rides make her dizzy. I know she's got no game for picking up men. I know she wants a dog someday but that it must come from a rescue. I know she's got a quirk about germs in hotel rooms.

I know she's smart. Has a great sense of humor. I know I'm happier when I'm around her. I know she's a game-changer.

Yet...

Sometimes I don't know her at all. Sometimes she's guarded. Puts a wall up. Gets nervous when I ask too many questions.

Sometimes she's like an entirely different person.

I know there's still something she's lying about.

What is it?

Perhaps she's just cagey after her last relationship. Perhaps she's anxious about where this is going.

Except it's something more than that. Something else. Something I'm not getting.

Maybe she's in massive amounts of debt or gets sacked a lot. She's a mediocre tour guide, if I'm honest. She didn't play any of the scheduled company videos she was meant to during the bus rides. There were a few basic answers she didn't have for guests. She was more nervous than confident most of the trip—anytime she was in charge, really.

But she said she was new at this, didn't she? Design is what she normally does. Or wants to do.

Perhaps she changes her mind often?

She's twenty-six. Perhaps she's not ready for the things I'm ready for.

I don't give a toss about any of that other shite. There's no amount of debt she could have that I couldn't pay off without a second thought. She can take all the time in the world to decide what she wants to do with her career. She can design or she can blog or she can open up a goddamned bakery shop for all I care.

I can be there for her while she figures those things out.

If she wants me to be.

I sure as fuck wasn't ready to commit to a relationship when I was her age. Hell, I wasn't ready last week.

She could move in with me. Of course she could—my house is bloody big enough for twelve. The second I have the thought, the idea of spending another night in it alone, without Daisy, is intolerable.

The fact that I've not renovated it yet feels like kismet. She's passionate about design—she'd want to oversee it herself, wouldn't she? It's fate. And as far as I'm concerned Daisy can do whatever she wants to the place.

I'll hire her to renovate it. Give her a reason to come to London. It'll take her an age to do it. A year at least. Massive pile.

I won't even care if her style is dreadful, or if she insists on installing an American refrigerator big enough to walk in. Or turns bedrooms into walk-in closets and mounts a telly on the wall in every room.

We'll sort it out this evening.

You know what happens to the best-laid plans, right?

CHAPTER TWENTY-SIX

Jennings

We're at the Liberty Bell when Nan starts to tire. She doesn't say anything but I see it. Most of the time she's so bloody energetic you've got to make sure she doesn't zoom off without you. But she assures me she's fine, so we carry on. She's been going full tilt all week, I'm sure she's looking forward to relaxing at Aunt Poppy's.

Daisy's fidgety. She got a call as we were touring Independence Hall. She stepped outside to take it and I didn't see her again until we'd finished that location and were crossing Chestnut Street.

We have a final group dinner tonight. It promises to be as tedious as the others we've had this week, though Daisy's promised tonight's has proper silverware, so at least there's that. I'd prefer having her to myself tonight, but as the guide she's obligated to attend the farewell dinner.

I'll take her for drinks afterwards. She can order that ridiculous champagne cocktail and tell me she's a sure thing. I laugh. How the hell was that only a week ago?

I need to find out how soon she can pack up and join me in London. I can arrange to have all her shit crated and shipped over if she's attached to it. I'd be content with tossing her on the plane with whatever she's got with her, but women are fussy creatures.

I get an email with her employment file from Rhys as the tour is wrapping up. The local guide, Gary, has led us to Franklin Square, which is our final stop. We've gathered at a fountain in the center of the park while Gary gives a brief history of the location, the group listening intently through their headsets. Daisy's stepped some fifteen or twenty feet away to take another call.

I'm half listening to Gary as he talks about the extensive renovation required to make the fountain operational again after it fell into disrepair in the nineteen seventies. He's a great guide, engaging and comfortable with public speaking. He's reading the group's interest level and tailoring his approach at each stop. Confident in what he's doing.

Unlike Daisy.

I need to ask Aunt Poppy who's in charge of training for this division when I see her tomorrow. Something is off here. Corners are being cut somewhere. Daisy's a sharp girl and charming on a one-to-one basis—but she's lacking in presentation skills and tour knowledge. It's troublesome that we'd not provide more training before putting her on a tour by herself. I should have paid more attention to it this week, but fuck it if I wasn't distracted by her.

We don't normally employ guides this young, either. Not unless they're exceptional. Not for a tour like this, one filled with a majority of older guests. The younger, less experienced guides would normally start on the adventure tours. Ones with high activity and a younger crowd.

Daisy ends her call and takes over for Gary as he says his goodbyes. She's reminding the group of the route back to the hotel and the meeting time for dinner. Pointing out gift shops and a carousel in the park. Places to get coffee or a light lunch. She seems fairly enthusiastic about Philadelphia. Comfortable, maybe? Or relieved her job this week is nearly done?

I open the email with a tap of my thumb. There's a file attached with Daisy's name on it and a note from Rhys that I skim through.

A home address placing her in Naperville, Illinois. Date of birth placing her at twenty-six. A hire date of... five years ago?

She's been working for Sutton Travel for five years? How?

Didn't she say this was a new job for her? That she started after her design job went bust? Isn't that what she said? I glance at her speaking to the group. She doesn't have her notebook today. It's the first time I've seen her without it.

I run a hand over the back of my neck to relieve the building tension as I pace. A new tour, she said, which I knew was a lie the moment it left her mouth. This tour has been on the schedule for years. A new tour for her, perhaps?

How in the hell did she get hired at twenty-one, though?

I turn my attention back to the email from Rhys.

Exemplary employee, it says. *Consistently high ratings from tour guests. Requests for repeat bookings with her specifically as their guide.*

In all honesty—that doesn't sound accurate. And I'm sleeping with her. I read on with growing trepidation. She started as an intern, Rhys notes. A position that didn't exist, but she sent a presentation to the head of the division making a case for herself. Created her own unpaid internship and convinced the company to hire her. She spent a summer shadowing the best tour guides we have. The division head was so impressed with her she had a job offer waiting when she finished college.

That explains the timing. In part. It explains how someone her age is five years in, but what about the rest of it? Who puts in that much effort to land a job they're not passionate about? It doesn't add up to the Daisy I've just spent a week with.

Then something else catches my eye.

Arizona State.

She graduated from Arizona State. With a degree in hospitality. Not urban planning. And I'm not too fucking British to know it doesn't snow in Arizona. It's the goddamned desert.

Snow, she said. Frost. Ice. One of those things. She left early for class to allot time for the weather. Slipped and ripped open her trousers.

Disgusted, I stop reading and slip the mobile into my pocket.

She's laughing at something Mrs. Delaine is saying. Behind her, the wind catches one of the jets of water in the fountain and the drops of water spread through the air like tiny crystals.

She's beautiful. A beautiful, deceitful little liar.

Or possibly crazy.

Who lies like that? For what purpose? Was this all a joke to her? Am I a joke to her? Or was it a lie that started in a hotel bar that she decided to keep running with? Or something she regularly does to amuse herself?

Who in the bloody hell is this girl? What's true and what's a lie? She can't have gone to university in both the snow and the desert. She can't have majored in both urban planning and hospitality. She can't have worked as both a tour guide and a designer during the same time periods.

I knew she was lying about something. I knew something was off, but I ignored my better judgement. Thought perhaps it was something small or silly like a history of getting sacked or possibly an arrest for public drunkenness during uni. That sort of thing.

Small lies, not a complete misrepresentation of who she is.

She catches me staring at her and winks. She goddamned winks at me. I nod once in response and I can feel my jaw ticking from the strain of keeping my response to a simple nod. I need time to think before I talk to her.

CHAPTER TWENTY-SEVEN

Jennings

"Where would you like to have lunch?" Nan and I are taking a leisurely walk back to the hotel. I offered to hail a taxi, but Nan would have none of it, insisting it's a lovely day for walking.

It is nice out and she seems to have regained her usual pep, so walking it is. It's less than a mile to the hotel and Nan said she'd like to take another walk through the parks we passed on our walking tour.

"I don't mind, Jennings. Wherever you'd like."

That's not exactly true. She's quite particular, but I nod and keep an eye out for a Nan-suitable restaurant.

"Wait, there is something I'd like to do." She stops walking and looks around as if to ascertain what direction we're walking.

"Sure," I agree, already pulling out my mobile to locate her request using GPS. "What is it?"

"I'd like cheesesteak."

"A cheesesteak?" Surely I've misunderstood. Nan is not a cheesesteak type of grandmother.

"Yes. I'd like to go to the Reading Terminal and have a proper cheesesteak."

I grin in reflex, my first thought being how much Daisy would enjoy the phrase 'proper cheesesteak' before remembering that when it comes to Daisy I should be doing a runner, not thinking about things that would make her smile.

"All right then, a proper cheesesteak it is," I agree while consulting my mobile. "Reading Terminal is a market of some sort?" I question as I open the maps app. "You've been before, have you?"

"I have. Before you were born, I think it was."

"That's quite a long time ago then, isn't it? High time you had another."

We take a right onto Arch Street while Nan tells me about her trip to the States with my grandfather some several decades ago. They used to travel quite a bit and she misses it, misses him, I'm sure. When he passed my cousins and I began our tradition of taking her on a trip each year. This is my second rotation, as it were.

"Tell me how you and Grandfather met. I don't think I've ever heard the story."

"No?" We're stopped at the crosswalk at 8th and Arch waiting for the light to change. She turns to me and gives me an appraising look. "Well I suppose you're old enough now," she finally says.

I can't help but laugh. "Why, Nan, was your courtship quite the scandal?"

"Courtship? There wasn't one. I knew my parents would object so we eloped before they had the chance."

"How have I never heard this story before?"

"I don't think your own father's heard this story."

"Well, let's have it then. I'll be gutted if you hold out now."

We walk and Nan talks. Tells me all about having met my grandfather when she was a sheltered eighteen and he was a handsome rogue in his mid-twenties. She was madly in love with him but knew her parents would not approve of the match, so she convinced him to elope.

"You convinced him?" I question.

"I was quite convincing in my youth, yes."

I grin and let her continue, sure that I want to press for added details on that.

She tells me that upon their return her mother was distraught that she'd missed her only child's wedding, so her father insisted they pretend to be engaged, not married. Promised he'd give his new son-in-law a position at the travel company he'd just founded. Set them up with a good start for their married lives if they'd play along.

"And did you? Play along?"

"We did," she says with a sigh. "It seemed the sensible thing."

"Well done then. A happy ending for all."

"Eventually yes. But they made me live at home for four months while we sorted the faux wedding. Your grandfather was obviously not welcome to stay, not in those days. I had a handsome new husband and we had to sneak around for the first four months of our marriage."

I cough a laugh into my fist as I hold the door for her at the Reading Terminal. It's a chaotic market of some kind. Indoors with booths one after another. Food, flowers, coffee, sweets—and that's just what I can see from the entrance.

"This is where you wanted to lunch?" I double-check. Perhaps the place has changed in the forty years since she's last been.

But Nan is beaming and looks like she's no intention of turning around now. So we find an empty wooden table—no small feat. Nan holds the table while I grab two Philly cheesesteaks and as many napkins as I can carry. Then we eat messy cheesesteaks with our hands and it makes Nan so happy that I don't even mind not having proper utensils. Or a plate.

When we're done eating we walk around the market. Nan stops to buy a trinket or two while I run the information from Rhys' email over and over in my mind, comparing it to everything I know—thought I knew—about Daisy.

It doesn't make any sense.

It's like two different people.

Maybe she's mentally disturbed? Off her meds or something? I rub my thumb across my bottom lip as I think. She doesn't come across as a nutter though. No more so than most.

I check the time on my mobile as we exit the market onto 12th Street, wondering if I'll have time to talk to Daisy before this blasted group dinner this evening. I have so many questions for her. Why I think I'll get honest answers I've no idea.

"How far to the hotel do you think, Jennings?" Nan is glancing up and down 12th, trying to place our present location in relation to the hotel.

"Let me take a look," I respond as I open the map app on my mobile. "Are you ready to admit you're tired? Shall I sort a ride back?"

I've got my head down, tapping the hotel information into my mobile as I speak, so I hear the tires screeching before I see the car. I look up in time to catch the impact but it's already too late.

CHAPTER TWENTY-EIGHT
Violet

Where the hell are they? The entire group—minus Jennings and his nan—are on the bus. We're about to leave for the final group dinner and they're late. I walk into the lobby and take another look around, casting a hopeful glance as the elevator doors open.

It's not them.

We were supposed to leave five minutes ago. I've been stalling, waiting on Jennings, but he's not here. They've not been late for anything this week, so they must not be coming.

Maybe I misunderstood something? Maybe he was taking his nan out for a special dinner tonight? I know Jennings hates the group dinners. That must be it. He said we'd have dessert after—which honestly could have meant sugar or sex, I'm not sure. But he did mention it, so maybe he meant he wouldn't see me at dinner?

That must be it.

Must be.

So why do I feel a sense of unease?

I make a final visual sweep as I exit the lobby. George is standing next to the open bus doors and he smiles at me as I approach. He's been trying to make a move on me all week. Well, on Daisy. I feel like an asshole for rejecting him. I know he's got to be confused about the cold shoulder I'm giving him when as far as he knew he was on good terms with Daisy. I hate feeling like I'm in the middle—even if it was a casual thing between them. It makes me feel responsible for his confusion when I'm not. Or maybe I am, since I'm the one delivering the rejection. Daisy said it was just sex between them, but he did switch tours with someone else to be here—to see her.

So maybe he likes her more than she knows. Or maybe he just wants to get laid. What do I know?

Maybe Jennings just wanted to get laid?

Jesus, Violet, I silently lecture myself. I'm the one who just wanted to get laid. That's what started this mess. I wanted a simple no-strings-attached one-night stand. I'm the one who smiled at Jennings and told him I was a sure thing. I'm the one who ran out the door the next morning.

I cannot be upset if he disappears now.

I cannot.

That's what I wanted in the first place.

Except…

I don't want that anymore. I gnaw at my bottom lip as I take a seat on the bus. By the time the bus is in drive—less than a minute later—I'm in full-on panic. I did run out that morning—the morning we met. Maybe he's returning the favor now?

Holy shit, I'm a nutcase.

Nut. Case.

I remind myself that I saw him five hours ago and everything was fine. I remind myself of this all the way to the restaurant. And through dinner. And the return drive to the hotel.

By the time the last of the guests says goodnight and leaves the lobby I'm not so sure that I'm crazy. By the time my hotel room door shuts behind me my heart is officially beating faster than normal.

You know that sick feeling you get when you know someone has let you down? You've got no proof of it exactly, but your heart knows.

Then you waste a lot of time waffling. Should you prepare yourself for the inevitable? Or hold out hope until not a moment of hope is left and let the disappointment crush you like a ton of bricks?

My room is quiet. I can hear the noise of the city just outside but the silence inside my room is deafening.

Or perhaps that's the silence in my head.

Why am I so leaveable? Am I really getting dumped by insinuation—again? We're not even going to have a conversation? He's just gone?

The worst part is this hurts more than when Mark did it. I spent two years with Mark and this hurts more.

So much more.

Just once it would be nice to get the 'it's not you, it's me' speech.

No. Stop it, I chastise myself. I'll see Jennings at breakfast tomorrow. This is a misunderstanding. I did not imagine this week. I did not imagine myself in love with him. I did not.

The knock on the door has me spinning around, relief pouring from me like an open wound. The feeling immediately following relief is remorse—for doubting him. A bit of embarrassment at my runaway thoughts. Of course he came.

Then I open the door.

But it's not Jennings.

CHAPTER TWENTY-NINE

Jennings

The brakes squealed as the car tires skidded across the asphalt. That's the first sound I noticed, the screams following suit. Odd how memory plays in slow motion when the reality happened so bloody quickly.

The car was slowed by a lamp post, coming to a stop just over the curb. The lamp post, however, couldn't withstand the impact. It toppled into scaffolding covering the front of the market, which in turn collapsed.

One of the metal scaffolding tubes hit Nan in the head when it fell. The rest is a blur of sirens and lights. Nan was loaded into an ambulance, insisting she was fine as blood seeped through the cloth the paramedics pressed to her head. She passed out briefly en route to the hospital—it was the only time she wasn't insisting she was fine.

My memento from the incident was eight stitches on my forearm while Nan was getting a CT scan. And now we're arguing over her staying the night in hospital.

"We're keeping you overnight," the doctor states and Nan tsks.

"But we have a flight in the morning," Nan says as the doctor and I both stare at her, unimpressed with her objections.

"Mrs. Anderson, you've had a head bleed and you're

on a prescription blood thinner. You're staying overnight for observation."

"You're definitely staying," I tell her. She's a stubborn lady but she's not winning this one. It took two staples to close the gash on her head, if the doctor thinks she should stay she's staying. "I'll extend our stay at the hotel and cancel our flight. I'll rent a car and drive you to Connecticut when you're released. Bethany can't be much more than three hours from here. It'll be less taxing on you than a flight."

The doctor is on my side so Nan gives up that fight, thankfully. By the time she's properly admitted and moved to a private room, visiting hours have passed. Once I'm certain she's settled and in need of nothing I tell her I'll be back in the morning and take my leave.

The adrenaline of the past hours allowed me to put Daisy out of my mind for a bit. But now I'm headed back to the hotel and worried what she must think.

We've missed the final group dinner, obviously. I'm sure Daisy is wondering what's become of me. And I'm still wondering what the everloving fuck to make of her.

I lost my mobile when the scaffolding came down, which has made the afternoon a royal pain in the arse, but at least I'm unable to torture myself by reading the email from Rhys over and over.

Doesn't matter much, as I'm fairly certain I've already committed every lie to memory.

Thankfully I've got my laptop back at the hotel. I'll email my assistant in London and ask her to cancel the flights to Connecticut and rebook my flight back to London. Arrange a car. Message Aunt Poppy and let her know not to meet us at the airport.

Change of plans.

But first things first.

Daisy.

I'm mad to get back to her. To talk, to make sense of this. The girl I spent the week with is real—I know she's real. I know the connection we have is real.

I know I'm falling in love with her.

With the version of her that I spent the week with, at least.

Yet I'm conflicted, because it doesn't look good. The inconsistencies—the lies—don't make sense. The entire thing leaves me with a sense of unease. A feeling of dread that she won't be able to explain this.

But no use putting the cart before the horse, is there? I've reached the hotel. I'll simply talk to her and clear the matter up one way or another. I stop at the front desk to extend the stay on both Nan's and my rooms, then bypass the elevator for the stairs. Daisy's on the second floor and the stairs will be quicker.

A decision I regret moments later. Though perhaps I shouldn't. Perhaps I should be grateful I caught them as I rounded the corner. Grateful I caught them at all. I was almost too late. Seconds later and I wouldn't have seen them. I'd have knocked on her door, unsuspecting.

Would she have answered?

Stuffed him in a closet perhaps? Swung the door open and smiled in my face? Or simply ignored the knock altogether?

I'll never know.

Just as well.

Because George has beaten me to Daisy's room—a handful of daisies in his hand. The door opens and she reaches out, grasping his forearm and yanking him into the room. The lock clicks into place as the door shuts and the echo feels like a bullet to my bloody heart.

It was too good to be true, wasn't it? I overreached

thinking it was something it wasn't. Thinking she was someone she wasn't.

CHAPTER THIRTY
Violet

I'm positive my expression is one of surprise, which is stupid. I should have expected this. I should have done more to stop this from happening. My shoulders slump and I reach out and yank him inside, shoving the door closed behind him.

The gig is up. The week is over. I'm going to have to trust George not to report Daisy for this scam, because I can't not tell him. Not when he's standing in my doorway with flowers.

Daisies.

The door clicks shut behind him and I run through the apology through my head. When I turn to deliver it he's closer than I expected. Way closer. Attempting to kiss me closer. I shove him off immediately.

"Hey! I said you could come in, I didn't say you could kiss me."

"Oh." He looks surprised and holds his hands up in apology as he takes a step back. "Sorry."

We stare at each other, the mood tense from the rejected almost-kiss.

"I'm confused, Daisy. I thought we had fun together."

"We did," I agree, although I'm unsure why the words are coming out of my mouth. I don't know what went on between George and Daisy, not really. She said it wasn't serious, but maybe it was for him?

But no, he's not looking at me the way Jennings looks at me. Not even close. They might have fun together and it was sweet of him to bring flowers, but he's just a guy wondering what happened to his friend with benefits.

A perfectly nice guy, I'm sure. But that's it.

My sister deserves someone who looks at her the way Jennings looks at me, so change of plans. I'm not telling George the truth. I'm breaking up with him. If it pisses Daisy off, too bad—she shouldn't have sent me in her place this week to begin with.

Although I wouldn't have met Jennings if she hadn't. The thought is like a punch to the gut, as is the one that immediately follows it. The one reminding me I don't know why he didn't show up tonight and we might be through.

"We did have fun, but I'm seeing someone now," I tell George with what I hope is a compassionate get-the-fuck-out smile. "I should have been more clear about that," I add and trail off, assuming he can fill in the obvious. *I'm seeing someone, so I'm not sleeping with you. Have a nice night.*

"The British guy?"

I nod.

"You just met him." George is unimpressed.

"When you know, you know," I quip, but I realize it's true.

"I didn't think you were into that."

"Into what? Love?"

He shrugs. "Yeah."

"Thanks." My tone is sarcastic. "Well, I am. Sorry to put an end to your Historic East Coast tour booty call." I say it a little sharply because fuck him. Any guilt I felt about interfering is gone. Daisy deserves better.

"I didn't think you were a serious kind of girl, that's all." He has the decency to look chagrined as he says it.

It makes me wonder if it's harder being Daisy. Being the fun twin. I always thought it must be easier, but maybe not. She's not as cautious as me. She dives into things, into relationships. She takes risks and assumes the best out of everyone. But it doesn't mean it's easier for her.

It doesn't mean it doesn't hurt when she's not taken seriously. It doesn't mean she doesn't deserve something more. Something real.

I walk George to the door and spend the rest of the night convincing myself that I'm going to see Jennings in the morning.

I don't believe it though.

CHAPTER THIRTY-ONE

Jennings

"Thanks for picking me up," I tell Rhys as I sling my bag into the boot of his Tesla. He slams the lid and wraps his arms around me in his typical American bear hug, slapping me on the back with enthusiasm. I pat his back half-heartedly and glance at his car. "New?"

"Yeah. Got it when I made the move to Vegas. You want to drive it?"

"No, Rhys, I'm drunk."

"From the plane?" He shakes his head in judgement. "They don't even have any decent liquor on board."

He's not wrong. But I made do just the same.

"It's not yet three o'clock and you're drunk on cheap liquor," Rhys summarizes as he looks me over. "And you didn't bring your new lady friend."

"My lady friend?" I glare in his direction but he likely misses it, as I slipped shades over my eyes the moment I cleared the automatic doors and stepped outside. Bloody desert is brighter than the surface of the sun. "You're a tosser."

"Daisy," Rhys says as if he needs to clarify. As if I have multiple lady friends, Jesus.

"Do you have any bourbon at your suite? Better yet, have the hotel bars been stocked yet?" I ask as I open the passenger door. The queue of cars picking up passengers at McCarran is three deep and the shrill whistle of security attempting to manage the chaos is not helping my mood.

"Plenty of liquor, I promise you," Rhys tells me as he slides behind the wheel. "How's Nan?"

"She's fine." I slump in the seat and get comfortable, flipping the visor down to block out the sun. "The hospital kept her one night as a precaution but she's fit as ever. Dropped her off with your mum yesterday. Slept in your old bedroom and your mum made me pancakes for brekkie."

"Lucky bastard."

"She sent biscuits for you. They're in my bag."

"The shortbread?"

"The very same. I think she's worried about you."

"Worried? Why?"

"I believe she's concerned that you're living in a casino and hooking up with women of questionable moral character."

Rhys laughs. "My mother did not say 'hooking up.'"

"Nah, I think she just wants you to call more often. In any case I assured her you're still a virgin and that you'll call this weekend."

"Thanks. Owe you one."

We're silent as Rhys merges the car into traffic. Once we're past the airport loop and onto Swenson he asks again about Daisy.

"You bloody Americans are so nosey." I groan.

"I can tell you about the dancer of questionable moral character I fucked last night, if you prefer."

"Jesus, Rhys." I close my eyes behind my sunglasses and rub my temple, a headache already forming.

"So what happened? Talk it out, buddy. I thought this girl was going to make an honest man out of you."

"Honesty wasn't her strong suit, as it turns out."

"Ouch."

"Yeah."

He's silent once again and I'm hopeful that's the end of his inquisition. It's not, of course. Because hoping has nil to do with reality.

"So what I'm hearing is that you need more liquor before I get the story." Rhys taps his fingers against the wheel as we're stopped at a red light.

"Where should I start, you nosey fucker?"

"The beginning. And stop sighing at me like a little bitch."

"Fine," I agree. Then I try to recall where this week went so horribly wrong. "She was hiding something. From the very first night she was hiding something."

"As were you," Rhys points out like an annoying prick.

"Whose side are you on?"

"Don't be such a woman, Jesus. This chick's really got you wound up tight."

"You're right." The light turns green and we cross Tropicana Avenue. The Vegas Strip is a few streets to the left but impossible to miss. Daisy was impossible to miss too. "Let's walk the property so I can see what's been done since my last visit. I'll tell you the rest when I've had another drink."

We spend the better part of two hours walking around the new hotel. Vegas is the complete opposite of everything I'm used to. Massive and gaudy to my eye, but profitable, and that I can appreciate. The Windsor is set to open in just under a month. At just under two thousand rooms it's considered small by Vegas standards. A boutique behemoth. What a ridiculous oxymoron.

We picked up the property under two years ago.

Another developer had abandoned the project mid-construction, left near completion, but vacant. Viewing the property was eerie. An abandoned ghost town filled with untapped potential. Flash-forward to today and it's anything but still. Workers everywhere. Casino tables in place. Slot machines being delivered and rolled in as we watch.

Rhys found the property, convinced me and the board of the potential, and here we are. The original plans were reconfigured to fit our vision and our corporate brand. We were able to turn the property around much quicker by renovating what the previous owner had started as opposed to starting again with new construction.

"Well done, Rhys," I tell him as we make our way to the executive apartments. There's a separate floor with living quarters for the senior staff of the hotel, should they choose to live on site.

"Thanks." He runs me through the projected occupancy rate for the remainder of the year. Numbers well within reach. I've already run the numbers myself and am projecting this venture will become the highest source of revenue for our company within eighteen months.

But I'm not interested in business at the moment. This trip is superfluous business-wise. I came to drown my sorrows, truth be told. "Show me what Vegas has to distract me."

Rhys' eyes light up and he claps me on the back as the lift doors open ahead of us. "I know just the thing."

Famous last words.

Four-ish drinks later I'm telling him everything. He's taken me to some bar his buddy owns. In Henderson, for fuck's sake, but at least it's not a strip club. He offered, of course he did. He offered hookers too after I passed on the strippers and I wondered if possibly his mum wasn't right to be worried about him.

"So I go running back to the hotel like a fucking knob," I tell him. "We missed the farewell dinner due to the accident. It was late by the time Nan was admitted, so I'm rushing back to the hotel. Desperate to see Daisy even though she's clearly a bit of a nutter." We're sitting at the bar and I motion for another drink.

"Clearly." Rhys is doing his best to keep up with my drunken ramblings. He's a brilliant friend.

"And the wanker of a driver is going into her room."

"Ah." He winces in reaction to my misery.

"Right! The guy she said she'd nothing going on with. Walking into her room at quarter past ten in the evening."

"Lying whore." Rhys shakes his head in empathy.

"Don't call her that." I scowl at him and pound back the shot in front of me.

"Sorry." Rhys holds up a hand in apology. "I thought we hated her. Got it. We're not there yet."

"Maybe it was the driver she was trying to get back at. By picking me up that night. Do you think?"

"Maybe." He shrugs, because there's nothing much else to say, is there?

"I don't think it was normal behavior for her though. Picking me up in the bar. She was fairly awkward at it."

I sip at the bourbon I'm consuming between shots and try to run through the events in my head again. My memory is cloudy at present.

"Her pussy was fucking nirvana." I'm not certain what that has to do with anything but in my drunken state it feels important to mention. "And her mouth, bloody hell." I drop my head into my hands on the bar top.

"I'm not saying a word," Rhys mumbles before

tipping his own glass to his lips. He tossed his keys to the bartender an hour ago and settled onto the stool for the long haul of watching me get drunk and listening to my rambles.

"I think she misled me."

"With her magic pussy?"

"Yeah, exactly." I glance around. "Do they have any food in this bar? I think we should eat."

"Nah. We'll have the car swing through In-N-Out Burger on the way back."

"We don't have the keys, Rhys. And you can't drive a Tesla drunk. I know the damn thing drives itself, but that can't be allowed. If that's allowed, next thing you know people will be strapping their kids in and sending them to nursery in a car with no driver! Society has gone to hell." I shake my head and think about waving a fist in the air like an old man. Because I'm fucking old.

"Car service will pick us up," he replies, holding up his mobile. "When we're ready."

"Fuck," I groan. "I don't even have a phone. Lost it during the accident. My dick is dry and I've got no mobile." I glance back at the bar and knock back the remainder of my drink in one gulp and stand, albeit shakily.

"Okay, I guess you're ready now." Rhys taps a contact on his mobile with one hand and signals the bartender with the other.

CHAPTER THIRTY-TWO

Violet

I drop Daisy's suitcase in her entryway with a sigh of relief. Home, sweet home. Or home, sweet Daisy's couch in my case. Traveling sucks. Traveling while feeling sorry for yourself sucks even more.

So that's over.

The trip.

And Jennings.

I want to hate him, but I don't. I want to be angry at him for showing me something wonderful and then taking it away.

Fine. I'm a little angry. I kick off my shoes and grab a diet soda from the fridge before slumping onto the couch.

It was all a big fat lie anyway.

Because I'm a liar and I got what I deserved, didn't I? Still, I did my best to tell him the truth. As much as I could.

My feelings were real.

Daisy's apartment is so quiet I can hear her wall clock ticking. Tick, tick, tick.

He left without so much as a goodbye. I'm sorta numb about that. Like how in the hell does that happen to a girl twice? At least with Mark I was able to call him an asshole to his face. I had to leave Jennings a note, since I couldn't find him. I asked at the front desk if he'd checked out. They don't normally share information like that but they knew me as the tour guide. I played it off like I was worried about him getting to the airport and wondered if he'd checked out yet.

Nope. He *extended* his stay. His and his nan's.

So on my way to the airport I left a note for him at the front desk. Who even knows if he got it, but I felt good writing it.

Yet as I sit here I'm conflicted. I so badly want to make excuses for him. Understand what happened. Maybe something came up? An emergency? Maybe I misunderstood and I was supposed to meet him somewhere and I'm the one who didn't show up?

These crazy thoughts are swiftly followed by rational ones. The ones that point out none of that is likely. That he knew which room I was staying in. That he didn't leave a note for me at the desk. That he never picked up his phone. That he owed me nothing.

I've got no right to be upset.

I asked for a one-night stand and I got it. I cringe, remembering that I told him I was counting him as my one-night stand. I'm such an asshole.

I pop open the soda and wiggle the can tab back and forth until it pops off. I'm not sure why I do this. I don't like drinking out of the can if the tab is missing. It feels weird against my lips, unfamiliar. It shouldn't make the soda taste any different but it ruins the experience.

That's me. I'm an experience-ruiner.

Maybe he was lying too? Maybe he doesn't have a job either and lives on his nan's couch? He said he had his own place but hell, I said I was a tour guide. Maybe he's wanted by the law or has a terminal disease and didn't want to put me through the pain of losing him slowly.

Okay, fine. That's unlikely.

He wouldn't have made it through customs if he was a wanted felon and no one with a terminal disease has that kind of stamina.

Was it just an escape for him this week? From the real world? That's what he was supposed to be for me, when it started. One night where I pretended to be someone I'm not. Someone more like my sister. Outgoing and spontaneous and, well, easy.

Perhaps I was merely a convenient booty call, like Daisy was for George, and I'm an idiot for thinking it was something it's not.

Except... whatever it was we had became real for me, real fast. I thought it did for him too. I know it did. So he's either one hell of an actor or a coward.

Gah! That's probably it. He's a commitment-phobe. A thirty-six-year-old man with a job and his own place who looks like he does would not be alone if there wasn't something wrong with him.

I bet he's not even thirty-six. I bet he's *almost* thirty-seven. Ha.

Wow. I'm not good at throwing shade. Also, I'm not sure it counts as shade if I'm not saying it out loud. I suck.

As an added slap in the face to all of this, I have a job interview.

Next week.

In London.

We were in the middle of the walking tour in Philadelphia when the call came. I slipped outside to take it while the group toured Independence Hall, standing outside with the phone pressed to my ear and a huge grin on my face. It's a dream job for me. A dream bigger than I'd have ever dared dream if Jennings hadn't suggested it.

Pushed me, even.

It's with Sutton International—the parent company of the tour company Daisy works for—in their London offices. I applied for it earlier in the week when Jennings suggested moving up in the company. Of course I applied as an external applicant since I don't actually work for the company. But he'd gotten me thinking with the suggestion and I figured why not? There was no reason I couldn't apply as myself, as Violet. So I did. And I got the call.

When I answered and realized the call was from Sutton International asking for Violet I almost thought I was caught. As if they would call me on my cell phone to ask if I was impersonating Daisy. Silly.

The position is with their design and development department. I'd be working with the team that refurbishes and redesigns the hotels they acquire—for the European market. Historic properties in some cases. Visions of charm and period details danced in my head. I almost clicked my heels together as I spoke with the human resources representative.

I spent the rest of the day feeling like I had the best secret in the world. One I couldn't wait to share with Jennings, but there were too many people around. After dinner, I thought. I'd tell him after dinner. He'd be excited. I'd be in London—next week! I could see him again—next week! And if I get the job, I'd be able to see him all the time!

But I never got the chance to tell him any of that.

It's funny how feelings can go from solid to cracked in the matter of an instant. I was in. All in. Totally in on the idea of picking up and moving to London. For Jennings, but for me too. It's something I've always dreamed about, living overseas.

The interview is scheduled for Monday. If I even bother to go, that is. I should go. They're paying for my flight and two nights in a hotel. It'd be my first trip to London. Not much time to do more than interview, try fish and chips and purchase a souvenir magnet at the airport. But the idea of it is sort of tainted now. Not quite how I'd imagined it. Would going be wasting their time? I'm not a time-waster. And I'm not a hundred percent certain I could take the job if it was offered.

Also, I have another option. I have an interview on Friday with a local company. It's a good fit for me. A great commute. Well, since I don't have a home at the moment I suppose the commute is irrelevant. But the job is about a half hour from Daisy's place. The pay is great—about ten percent more than I was making before, plus a bonus structure. I could be back on my feet pretty quickly with this job—and back in my own place.

Two weeks ago I'd have been jumping for joy about the possibility of this job. It's a good fit. Everything I was looking for. A good move, career-wise. A safe choice.

But now? Now I want more. I want an adventure. I want to push myself, take a chance. Spread my wings further than a thirty-mile radius of where I was born. But can I? Without love as an added incentive?

Do I have the guts to move overseas by myself? It's insane. A totally insane idea. It's a Daisy kind of idea, I think with a smile. I pick up my phone to call her, but as I'm thumbing through my contacts to dial, the phone rings. It's her.

"I was just about to call you," I say by way of hello.

"Twin win!" she replies. "Beat you to it."

"You did. By about three seconds."

"Are you home yet?"

"Yup. Sitting on your couch and drinking your soda."

"Good. Rest of the tour go okay? You survived? You don't hate me for making you go?"

"I survived. It was possibly even good for me."

"Was that hard for you to admit?"

"A little bit. What about you? What's going on with your frenemy?"

"Why, what did you hear?"

"What would I have heard?" I make a face even though she's not there to see it. "Was Mom supposed to update me on your sex life?"

"Haha. No, I guess not. What about your British lover? Did you elope? I won't be mad if you did. Just throwing that out there. Random FYI."

"Err, no. We definitely did not elope." I try to sound breezy when I say it, but I fail. Miserably.

"That sounds foreboding. What happened?"

I take a deep breath and bring her up to speed.

CHAPTER THIRTY-THREE

Jennings

"Is your asshole cousin still here?"

I look up from the laptop before me at the sound of Canon's voice. "Still here," I call out, though he's speaking to Rhys. "Still your boss as well," I add.

"Is he done sulking?" Canon asks Rhys, ignoring me, though I know damn well he heard me. "I can't watch the game with that kind of energy." He's so full of shit. He rounds the corner of Rhys' hall carrying a couple of pizza boxes and grins, pretending surprise at seeing me. "Oh, my bad. You are here."

"Fuck off."

"You look well." The pizza boxes hit the coffee table with a thud before he grabs himself a beer from the fridge. I can't possibly look well, so I'm certain that comment is an attempt at being clever. "Did I miss kickoff?" he asks as he tosses the beer cap in the direction of Rhys's kitchen counter, where it bounces until it hits the tiled backsplash and comes to a stop.

This setup they've got is like some goddamned American-style frat house. But with room service, valet parking, and a five-minute commute to work. I'd seriously doubt their ability to run this hotel if I didn't know better. If I hadn't seen them at work with my own eyes.

Still.

My eyes narrow as Canon drops onto the sofa and flips the lid on one of the boxes. It's hard to believe these idiots are capable of anything when I see them like this, much less that they're integral executive staff. Hence the onsite living accommodations-turned-frat party.

"Did you ask the bar to send up another bottle of bourbon?" Rhys says. See what I mean? They've got access to a bar with delivery. A bar with an unlimited tab, the fact that the bourbon is for me notwithstanding.

I should break it to Aunt Poppy that Rhys is never moving back to Connecticut, because as far as I can tell these assholes are going to live in this hotel until their dicks fall off. I'm positive I passed a stripper in the hallway yesterday entering someone's suite. Or possibly a hooker, but I'm choosing to believe she was the former.

I asked Rhys and Canon if I should be worried about the going-ons here, which they assured me was unnecessary. And now I'm the arsehole.

Fucking Americans.

I pour myself a drink as the two of them sprawl on the sofa and turn the volume up on the game.

I tune them out and go back to reading Daisy's employment file on my laptop. Again. It just doesn't add up. I've already read her performance reviews. I can't find any obvious inconsistencies. Her degree from Arizona State is legitimate. So she lied about going to Penn. The guide positions are contract, but she's consistently worked for the last four years. So she lied about working in design. I can't see how it's possible she'd have had the time to do both.

But why?

Why tell me she was recently hired as a guide? That lie doesn't make any sense. None of them do, but this one sticks out as especially unnecessary. Unless it was to set up the lie about losing the job. About dating her boss and getting let go. A person would have to be borderline psychotic to lie that deeply.

There's something here I'm not seeing.

The note she left me said I was an arsehole. "You're a special kind of arsehole," she'd written. I'm not sure if she thought I wouldn't get it if she'd written 'asshole' or if it got her off to use the British spelling, but either way I'm unsure how I'm the one at fault.

She's certifiably crazy.

I groan and toss my laptop aside.

"You're bringing down my chi, bro." This from Canon. He holds the pizza box open in front of me and I take a slice because combining top-shelf bourbon and shitty pizza is the least of my issues at present.

"You wouldn't know chi if it was sucking your dick," I tell him. He really wouldn't. Canon is not a zen motherfucker.

"Finally!" He tosses the box back onto the table and raises his hands in victory. He's still holding a beer in one of them and I expect a mess, but he's apparently well-trained in gesturing with drink, as he doesn't lose a drop. "I knew you had a sense of humor in there somewhere. No." He shakes his head. "No, that's a lie. I didn't believe it. But Rhys said you did and I believed him."

"Thanks," I say drily. I couldn't give a fuck if I'm pissing him off with my foul mood.

"What are you working on?" Rhys asks, removing his eyes from the game long enough to side-eye the open laptop. He knows damn well what I'm working on.

"Still looking at that employment file you sent. Trying to make sense of it."

"Make sense of what?" Canon asks. He's a nosey

bastard on the best of days, which suits his position as head of surveillance, but makes him annoying to deal with.

"My guide last week. Nothing she told me matches with her employment file. I thought perhaps her employment history was falsified, but everything seems in order."

"That's a security issue," Canon replies as he swipes my laptop off the couch and starts scanning through the open document. "Daisy Hayden," he reads aloud. "For starters, she sounds hot."

"Be respectful, Canon. He's still in love with her," Rhys tells him. I shoot him a dirty look, which he misses as his attention is on the telly.

"All I'm saying is a woman named Daisy is bound to be a good time."

I rub my temple with my index finger. I think I feel a headache coming on.

"Okay, let's see what we have to work with." Canon taps on the touchpad as he scrolls through the documents. I should have asked him to look at this two days ago, come to think of it. His fingers begin flying across the keyboard as he opens programs I'm not sure I have access to. Hell, I'm not sure he's even using the company database right now.

"How are you accessing that?"

"Don't ask."

I don't. Instead I fill him in on what I do know.

"Her background checks out. No arrest records. No tax issues. Good credit rating." More rapid typing, then a pause as he turns the computer in my direction. Her employee ID is on the screen. "This is her?"

"Yeah."

He flips the computer back around and types

something else. "Her address checks out. The lease is in her name. One-bedroom apartment in Naperville, Illinois. Looks like a nice place." He shrugs.

"Yeah, she said she lived there. That part is true, I think."

"Excellent performance reviews."

"That part I have an issue with. She was an average guide at best. Nervous. Forgot a few things."

"Maybe she's sleeping with her boss," Canon offers.

"Too soon," Rhys pipes in from across the couch.

Canon nods and keeps reading. I down the rest of my drink and watch the team on the telly score, though to be honest I'm not paying enough attention to even know who's playing.

"Who is Violet Hayden?"

"Who?"

"The emergency contact on her employment records is listed as Violet Hayden."

"Fuck if I know. She never mentioned a Violet. Her sister? Mother maybe?" Who gives a shit?

More typing, then Canon is grinning. I don't think I've ever seen him so amused. "Certificate of live birth. State of Illinois," he announces.

"Jesus Christ, did she lie about her age?" An overwhelming sense of dread consumes me. "She's not underage, is she? I asked. She looked young but not that young. Bloody hell."

"She's twenty-six," Canon confirms, giving me a look like I'm some kind of creep.

"Yeah, she said she was twenty-six. What's your point?"

"It was a twin birth." He says this slowly, as if it has meaning.

"Okay." I stare at him a moment, letting that sink in.

So she has a sister. She mentioned a sister. Canon seems to find this more fascinating than I do though, so I feel as though I'm missing something. And perhaps I didn't need that last drink.

Canon's typing again. "Penn, degree in urban planning," he tells me and makes a waving gesture with his hand as if I'm supposed to reply.

"Yes, that's what she said."

"Was employed as a junior designer until six months ago when the company she was working for was bought out." He says this bit slowly, as if—

Holy hell.

They switched places.

I lean forward and brace my elbows on my knees and rub both palms over my face. I wasn't with Daisy at all. I was with Violet. I run her name through my mind a few times as memories of her flash behind my lids. It all fits, doesn't it? She was telling me the truth. Sort of.

"Why?" I finally sputter. "Why in the hell would they do such a thing?"

"Hell if I know. That's your problem, not mine."

I recall her notebook. How nervous she was during the tour. I don't know why they did this, but I don't think they did it often. Why didn't she just tell me?

If they switched, everything she said to me was true. I recall asking her about the driver, if they were involved. The look of genuine surprise on her face followed by the denial. I recall her pointing at herself and saying no, she was not involved with him.

Her sister was though, wasn't she? That's it. It all falls into place. She didn't tell George about the switch either. No wonder the guy looked confused every time they were in the same room.

I really am a special kind of arsehole.

"Where is she? Violet?" I ask Canon after telling Rhys to sod off. "Do you have an address for her?"

More typing.

"No," he finally says. "One second. I'll figure it out. If people realized how easy this was to do they'd shit themselves." He says it gleefully, like it gets him off a little to cyber-stalk people. I make a note to be less of a dick to him in future.

I stand and pace while Canon searches. She can't be that hard to find, I reassure myself. I know where her sister is—if nothing else, I can camp out on her doorstep and demand she tells me where Violet is.

"Does she have your address?" Canon asks, his forehead wrinkled as he stares at something on the screen.

"No, I don't think so. I mentioned what street I live on, but nothing specific. Why?"

"She's in London."

Bloody hell.

I'm in the wrong place.

But I don't think she's in London for me.

"There was a job opening in the design group I mentioned to her. See if she applied."

"On it." Canon types as I pace. "She did. An offer to interview was extended and accepted. It's scheduled for tomorrow at ten."

Tomorrow at ten. Before I'm done doing the math Canon is already on it. "There's a direct flight leaving in two hours and twenty minutes. It'll get you into Heathrow at ten fifteen tomorrow morning. If there's no delay you can catch her before her interview is over."

"That should go over well," Rhys comments. "Since she still doesn't know who you are."

"Tiny insignificant issue," I tell him.

Rhys and Canon exchange a look.

"Okay. I'll book your seat while you take a shower," Canon announces. "Rhys, get the car from the garage. We'll meet you downstairs."

CHAPTER THIRTY-FOUR

Violet

London is glorious. Magical. It's everything I ever imagined and though I've been here only a handful of hours, I already feel at home. There's an instant connection between me and this city, no less than the kind of instant connection you get with some people. Like I had with Jennings.

No. I'm not going to let thinking about him ruin this. I'm not. I've only got one afternoon to explore. My interview is tomorrow at ten. I've no idea how long it will last, but surely they didn't fly me across the ocean for a forty-five-minute meeting.

Daisy convinced me I'd be crazy to pass up this interview and she's right. I still hate it when she's right, but I'm starting to appreciate that sometimes in life throwing caution to the wind is the best choice.

I've got today. No matter what happens, I've got today in London. I'm going to enjoy every minute. I'll take the Tube, I decide. Like a real Londoner. The St. James' Park station is just across from my hotel. I've already walked to Westminster Abbey and Big Ben. I've stopped for a coffee at Costa, just next to my hotel. And I've thought about how Mayfair is likely only a Tube ride away. That's where Jennings said he lived, wasn't it? Mayfair. I only remember such a random detail because my birthday is in May.

I stand in front of my hotel and toe the sidewalk with my sneaker while I debate. Then I check both ways—twice, because the direction cars drive in here is confusing—and cross the street. I get an Oyster card and I figure out the Tube map just like a real Londoner. It's only one stop to Green Park, which is on the edge of Mayfair, according to my map. I'll just walk around a bit, no harm in that. Assuming Green Park is an actual park and not a garden for a castle, I'm sure it's open to anyone to wander about.

That's my story anyway. If I'm randomly questioned about why I'm walking around Mayfair. Which is unlikely, but it's always good to have a plan when you're lying.

I exit the Tube station at Green Park and jog up the steps to the street, a smile already on my face. When I get to the top I have to refrain from spinning around in a circle like some weirdo reenacting a scene from *The Sound of Music.*

The park is straight ahead. The street is brimming with red double-decker buses and those oddly-shaped black cabs they use here. All the cars have long skinny license plates, and how is this all so charming? How is it possible for a city to give me butterflies?

I accept pretty quickly that I've no idea where the residential area of Mayfair might be, or where Jennings' apartment might be, if he even lives here. He could have been lying after all. And this area seems pretty swanky even to my naïve eye. As in, the Ritz Carlton is just ahead. But it doesn't matter. I don't even remember what street he said he lived on. I just wanted a general impression of the area, somewhere to place him when I remember him.

So I walk. I pop in and out of stores. I get my souvenir magnet and a box of cookies for Daisy. Except they're called biscuits, which makes them even better. I buy a ticket and ride a double-decker bus around the city. When I finally cave to the jet lag and head back to my hotel my heart is full and I'm glad I came.

The hotel has a pub called the Blue Boar and I stop there for dinner. It's a classic British pub. Sophisticated classic. Herringbone wood floors and green leather chesterfield sofas. I select a small round table in front of the windows and place my obligatory order for fish and chips. As I settle in to wait I cannot believe it was less than two weeks ago that I walked into a similar bar an ocean away with the intent of picking up a sexy stranger.

I'd never leave this bar with someone. It's so not my nature.

But I did leave with Jennings. Practically skipped out the door with him, didn't I?

Maybe I'll try being that carefree girl again, but not tonight. Tonight I'm regular old Violet because I don't need to pretend to be anyone else. Tomorrow I'm going to put on my own clothing—though I did nab the perfect earrings from Daisy—and nail this interview.

CHAPTER THIRTY-FIVE

Violet

I don't know what is happening, but today is my day. Maybe it's the water here or the hotel shampoo, but I'm having the perfect hair day. The kind that only comes along a few times a year and when it does you make the best of it and take a bunch of gratuitous selfies to use on your social media profiles.

I arrive at the Sutton International offices early. Too early, so I walk around a bit to waste some time. Showing up too early for an interview is just as inept as showing up late, so I'll stay outside until precisely ten minutes before my scheduled interview.

The offices are in Berkeley Square, which as it turns out is in Mayfair. I hadn't realized by looking at the address on paper, but as the cab wound its way through the London streets I figured it out. That, and I asked the cab driver.

So here I am, walking in the Berkeley Square Gardens, smack in the middle of Mayfair. I wonder if the magic of this place would wear off if I saw it every day? It's hard to believe it could. The architecture surrounding me is so inspiring. I could spend a lifetime admiring the roof lines from this spot in the park. Heck, even the gravel path beneath my feet inspires me. The wrought-iron fencing and the street lamps, the window casings and the stonework.

I can't imagine it getting old, not ever. I want to pinch myself to make sure being here is real and not a dream.

I look at the surrounding buildings and wonder if any of them are residential or if they're all offices.

And just like that I get a flutter in my stomach, thinking about how close Jennings *could* be. Thinking of him living or working in one of these buildings. He could cut through this very park to get to work.

Of course it's nearly ten, it's unlikely he's on his way to work at this hour. Unlikely I'd bump into him today. Unlikely I'd bump into him *ever*.

What would I even say to him? 'Hi, it's Violet, remember me? No, you probably don't since I told you my name was Daisy. Sorry about that. Nice to see you again. By the way, thank you for making me fall in love with you and then leaving without so much as a goodbye. See ya around, jerk.'

He really is a jerk.

How could he just leave like that? How? I know it was only a week, but the connection we had wasn't one you walk away from without a word. It was so much more than sex. We fit together, like finding a missing puzzle piece. One that you think you'll never locate and then bam, it's right there in front of you, just waiting to be snapped into place.

I don't know why I'm thinking about him again when he probably hasn't thought about me at all. It's nice to fantasize though, isn't it? Fantasy conversations are so satisfying. You always have the best comebacks and always get the final triumphant word. Jennings would grovel and have a really great explanation for standing me up. And I'd... well, I have no idea what I'd do. But I'd have to get the job and bump into him for this fantasy confrontation to happen, so I've got plenty of time to think about how I'd react.

Plenty of time.

***

I'm killing it in this interview. I've spent well over an hour with the hiring manager—the person I'd be reporting to directly if I got hired. We had an instant rapport and the more we talk the better it gets.

I love the vibe in the office too. Professional, yet comfortable. The building itself has an energy to it that makes me happy. It sounds crazy, but it's true. It's a lot like house-hunting. Sometimes you walk into a place and it just feels right.

This building feels right. The people feel right.

The hiring manager—Elouise—even asked me to grab a coffee with her before she introduced me to the rest of her team. We walked next door to a local coffee shop and ordered it to take away when we walked back to the office. People don't ask you to walk with them for coffee if the interview isn't going well.

I had this moment inside the coffee shop where I thought I saw Jennings and my heart stopped, but it wasn't him. Just a random hot-as-fuck British guy.

I love London.

And now I'm in the conference room with Elouise and three members of her team. We're reviewing a property they're currently renovating and they're asking my opinion. I'm not naïve, it's definitely part of the interview. But I'm in my element with this stuff, so it's fine. We're reviewing CAD drawings on an oversized wall monitor when the door opens.

It opens quickly, that's the first thing I notice. It's not

a timid opening of a door, one you'd expect when the room is occupied and the door closed. It's the opposite of that. Abrupt, as if the person is expected, but late.

The next thing I notice is the reactions from the table. Elouise is unfazed at the interruption, but the others all sit up straighter, the mood gone from relaxed to intent in a heartbeat.

"We're using the room," Elouise says after a pregnant pause. My back is to the door and I hear it shut behind me, but all of the energy in the room is still on that door so I assume whomever has arrived has stayed, not left. Across from me a man named Aaron adjusts the pen and pad in front of him so it's perfectly square.

"I wanted to sit in on this one," a voice says and it takes my entire body half a second to freeze. In fact, I'm fairly certain I could pass for one of those street performers who pretends to be a statue. Then I exhale. This is like the coffee shop, I'm sure. My imagination run rampant.

"You wanted to sit in on an interview for a designer?" Elouise asks, her tone unimpressed.

"Yes," comes the reply as he walks into view.

He looks just like Jennings.

Because it is Jennings.

CHAPTER THIRTY-SIX

Violet

Holy fuck. He's here. In London. In this conference room. My mind is spinning faster than I can process the thoughts, my heart racing as if I'm running a marathon.

He looks like shit. Tired and rumpled. Unshaven. Like he might have slept in what he's wearing. Yet somehow still perfect. Being in the same room with him feels as if a net of butterflies has been unleashed in my stomach. He's here. He's really here.

I remind myself that I'm having a perfect hair day. The kind of hair day every woman wants to have when she runs into her ex. It's possibly the dumbest possible thing I can think of right now but people react strangely in times of stress.

"Very well," Elouise says. "This is Violet Hayden. She's interviewing for the open design associate position on my team."

Wait.

Hold up.

If he's sitting in on an interview that means… that he works here.

See, those are the dots I should have been connecting when I was thinking about my hair. He works here. At the place where I'm interviewing. And last week he was on a tour where I told him I was the tour guide and my name was Daisy.

"Violet, this is Jennings Anderson. Our CEO."

I'm dead.

He's moved to the other end of the table across from Elouise and leaned over, extending his hand as if we've never met before. As if I'm a living, breathing person expected to shake his hand and say hello when clearly I. Am. Dead.

"Violet," he says, his eyes amused. I shake his hand. I don't even stand. I just shake it quickly and snatch my hand back, my skin tingling where we touched. What the hell is happening right now?

"I've had the opportunity to review Violet's CV," he says, looking directly at me. "Very impressive."

He knows.

He knows I'm Violet. He knows I impersonated Daisy.

A quick glance at Elouise as he tells her to continue with the interview and then he's back to watching me. Someone at the table coughs. There's a shuffling of papers and a click of a pen but Jennings simply sits with his eyes on me.

What is he doing? Why isn't he saying anything? Why is he allowing this farce to continue? I glance nervously around the room, waiting to see how this plays out.

Wait. Did he set this up? Did he bring me here just to humiliate me? Is that the game plan here?

Has he called the police and now he's stalling, waiting for them to arrive and arrest me? I wonder if I'll be extradited to the United States. I wonder if I want that or if the jails are nicer here? I wish I knew, but it's not likely I get a say so I guess it doesn't matter.

The interview carries on but I couldn't tell you a single question I've answered. I know I'm answering them. I know words are coming out of my mouth and the people around the table are responding to them with nods and additional questions. But I've got no clue what's being said. Not really. My eyes are darting over to Jennings every chance I get, my mind racing, trying to figure out what his game is.

Finally the interview draws to a close, Elouise laying out the next steps in the interview process. I smile and nod in all the right places between shooting furtive glances at Jennings, wondering why he's allowing this to continue. When Elouise stands I nearly exhale in relief, one hand on my bag and my rear already half out of my seat before Jennings speaks.

"I'd like a word with Miss Hayden."

CHAPTER THIRTY-SEVEN

Jennings

"I'll need the room," I announce without taking my eyes off of Violet. The three associate designers scatter so quickly their chairs spin. My mum isn't as quick. She stands slowly, with pointed glances between Violet and myself, and announces we'll talk later as she closes the door behind her.

"Violet." I say it because I like hearing her name on my lips. It suits her. I laugh, remembering how she tried to sell me on her name being Daisy. It feels like forever ago.

"Hi," she replies, her face unsure. She's nervous, her body tensed as if she's ready to do a runner. She can run as far as she likes. I'll follow.

"I'm sorry that I missed dinner," I say, realizing what a prize idiot I sound like the moment the words leave my mouth. "I'm sorry I left, is what I meant." I push my chair back and stand, moving to the chair beside hers. "Without talking to you. I'm sorry I let you out of my sight for even a moment."

"Oh," she says. "So you're not having me arrested?"

"Arrested? No." I laugh as I sit. She turns so we're facing each other. That's a start. "No. Not unless I can arrange to be locked inside the same cell as you." Tempting thought, if this doesn't go the way I've planned. "Besides, I didn't rush here from the airport to chase you off. I did it to catch you. To ask you to stay."

She blinks at me, the tension easing from her face. It's quickly replaced with a scowl. "I'm supposed to be telling you off right now."

"Sorry?"

"You left! You. Left. You made me fall for you and then you just left and broke my heart." Her voice catches when she says that and I feel like a right prick. "I had all these grandiose ideas of how cleverly I'd tell you off if I ever saw you again."

"I'm an idiot. I thought…" I trail off, unsure if I'm about to dig myself deeper.

"You thought what?" Her scowl game is strong. A lesser man would likely be intimidated. As it is, I'm apprehensive.

"I thought you'd lied."

"I did lie. A lot."

"About George."

"Oh." Her eyes widen. "Oh." Then she's shaking her head. "I'd never lie about that. I wasn't with him. Ever. But my sister was and he thought I was her."

"I know. I figured that out. Eventually."

"That's why you left? Instead of talking to me?"

"I fucked up."

"Agreed."

I need to touch her. It's killing me having her this close and not in my arms, but I settle for picking up her hand and she allows it.

"I'm sorry too," she says. "I'm sorry I told you my name was Daisy. Everything else I told you was true. My feelings were true. You must think I'm crazy."

She looks at me, and I see the vulnerability in her eyes. Her teeth sink into her bottom lip.

"You're exactly the kind of crazy I've been looking for my entire life."

She laughs. "Right."

"I'm quite serious, Violet," I tell her and she grins.

"Quite serious." She giggles. "I love how everything sounds so posh when you say it. You could get me to do just about anything when you say words like quite with that British accent."

"Good. Marry me."

That wipes the smile right off her face. Not quite what I'd intended. "What?" I'm glad she's sitting because she looks a little pale.

"Marry me."

"That's"—she pauses, sucks in a breath—"insane. We've known each other a week."

"So?" I realize I've missed a step of a proper proposal so I grab a paperclip from the conference table and bend it open, twisting it into a wonky circle as I kneel in front of her.

"Are you insane?" Her eyes are wide and she's shaking her head back and forth. "I wasn't questioning why you weren't on your knees. I was questioning how you could ask me to marry you when we barely know each other."

"I know enough, Violet. I'm asking because I'm sure. I'm sure of what we are when we're together. I'm sure that I can't live without you. I'm sure that I'm in love with you."

She sucks in a breath so I forge on.

"Our lives will be outstanding together, Violet—you and I—because I won't allow anything less for you. I'm all in. I'm the sure thing, Violet. When it comes to you, I'm the sure thing. You told me once that no one's ever asked. I'm asking. Marry me."

She blinks once, then again, and I wonder what she's

thinking. She takes the paperclip ring from my hand and stares at it, rubbing it between her finger and thumb but not putting it on.

"I'll get you a nicer one. Of course." God, she can't be thinking I expect her to wear that, can she? "Whatever you like. We'll pick it out together. We can be engaged as long as you like." No, that's a lie. "A few months," I clarify, and then when her eyes widen—"A year."

She doesn't say anything.

"You'll work here," I continue. "Take the job."

That seems to snap her out of her daze. But when she speaks I don't like what she has to say.

"No."

CHAPTER THIRTY-EIGHT
Violet

He's serious.

He's not messing with me. He's absolutely, completely serious. And that declaration took some balls.

"No?"

He doesn't even look bothered by the rejection. Not in a way that implies that he doesn't care. But in a way that implies he won't accept no as an answer, so it's irrelevant. He gets off his knees though and sits, his posture confident. As if this ends how he wants. His elbows are resting on his knees and he's leaning into me, invading my space. Trampling my thoughts. My heart long since breached.

"No, I'm not going to work for you. It's weird."

"Why is it weird? My entire family works together. Hell, my parents give each other lifts to work every morning. That was my mum who interviewed you, by the way. Stepmum, but she's the one who raised me. I had nothing to do with you getting this interview. You got this on your own. We don't fly people in for interviews if we're not keen. The job will be yours on your own merits."

I shake my head. "I don't think so. I love you, Jennings. It's insanity, but I do love you. More than I ever thought was possible, but I need a career separate from you. I won't have my entire identity wrapped up in you."

He kisses me then. One moment he's a foot away and the next his hand is behind my neck and he's pulling my lips to his. Softly at first. Then my lips part and his tongue invades and I don't know how I can be expected to resist him. But then he speaks, and he doesn't make me.

"Fine. You'll get another job. Somewhere in London. Or I'll relocate to the States if you prefer."

"You'll relocate?" I laugh. The idea is preposterous.

"Yes. If you leave I'll follow. Wherever you are, I'll be. I'll make it work."

"Are you for real? Is this really happening?"

"So that's a yes to the proposal, no to the job offer?"

"I don't know, Jennings. This is all so fast."

"Say yes for now. Give me that much. Say yes for now. I've had longer to think this through than you have. All night, in fact. On a very long flight in a shite center seat in coach because my friend Canon has a perverse sense of humour. Say yes for now and I'll ask again when you're ready. In three weeks or three months or three years. Whatever it takes to get you to agree to spend your life with me. Just say yes."

I stare at him, unsure how I could deny him anything. Unsure why I'd even want to.

"Yes."

EPILOGUE

Violet

I can do this.

Women do this all the time, and it's not as though it's even particularly difficult. I mean, I don't want to insinuate that anyone who can't figure this out is an idiot, but they're most likely idiots.

But maybe—just to be safe, mind you—I'll read the instructions one more time.

Five seconds. Got it.

The thing is, I got some tips from a blog after typing 'tips for taking a pregnancy test' into Google, and now I'm not sure if I bought the right test because tip number one was choose the right HPT. What in the hell is an HPT? I had a whole shelf to choose from at Waitrose and I don't recall seeing that on any of them. I grabbed one that promised rapid results and ninety-nine percent accuracy and put it in my basket next to the Dairy Milk buttons and the multipack of Jaffa Cakes because I'm probably pregnant and I deserve them.

Anyway, tip number one was choose the right HPT. The next tip was wait for the results. Duh. The post actually suggested I take a break and sip on a cup of tea or coffee while waiting. So dumb.

"Babe, can you bring me a cup of tea?"

"Violet, just pee on the stick. It's quite literally the

only direction on the box. I don't understand why you keep reading it over and over again, love." He tosses the empty box onto the vanity where it lands with a hollow thud.

Tip number three was check the expiration date on the test, which I've done of course, but the way they list the date before month in the UK still throws me a little.

"Does that test expire on the seventh of October or the tenth of July?"

"It expires on the seventh of October," Jennings says patiently. He's going to be such a good dad. "Two years from now," he adds with a bit of sarcasm.

"It could be twins, you know," I say, mostly just to mess with him. The confidence on his face falters a bit as he reaches over to pick up the box again. "There isn't a home test for twins. We'd have to wait until the first ultrasound to find out." Assuming they both showed up at the first ultrasound. My mom was six months along before they found the second heartbeat. Holy crap, it really could be twins.

"Right." He clears his throat. "Well, a twofer would be lovely."

"A twofer? Did you just refer to the idea of me carrying two babies at the same time as a twofer? As if I'm carrying a twin pack of chocolate biscuits?"

"Would you prefer I call it a twin win?" He shrugs, unbothered by my reply. "I'm almost forty, love. I'd be quite chuffed to hit the ground running with two."

Dammit.

I'm positive he ups the British word count when I'm on the edge of being cross with him. He knows it's my weakness. He can get away with just about anything if he tosses in words like 'knackered' or 'gutted' into a sentence.

It occurs to me then that I'm going to have a British baby.

Do you know what's great about British babies?

Everything.

I mean, I know they're basically the same as American babies, but they have super-cool names like Poppy or Pippa. Amelia or Isla. Oscar or George. Well, maybe not George. Then when they get around to speaking it's in a British accent and let me tell you, a child having a tantrum in Waitrose with a British accent is about a hundred times less annoying than a child having a tantrum in Wal-Mart in an American accent. It's a fact. Wait a minute...

Oh.

My.

God.

"They're going to call me Mummy." I say it as a matter of fact as I drop my pants and sit. I don't even care that Jennings is still standing in the bathroom with me because we've been married a while now and way past tiptoeing around one another in the loo. I hold out my hand for the stick and Jennings hands it to me.

"Er, yes. I suppose so. Though I'm certain we could teach them to call you Mom if you prefer it."

"No!" I shake my head. "Are you crazy? I get to be a mum!" I finish with the test and snap the cap over the absorbent tip before placing it on the counter. "Don't look at it without me!" I warn as I flush and wiggle my pants up, then wash my hands. Jennings wisely doesn't move from his position leaning against the wall. "Has it been sixty seconds yet?"

"More like fourteen."

"Oh."

I manage to keep my eyes on his for another three

JANA ASTON

seconds before I give up on patience and move to the counter, leaning over the test with my elbows braced on the counter and my chin resting on my hand. Jennings moves behind me, his arms bracketing mine as he leans in and dips his head next to mine.

"Don't distract me," I say, because when he's this close we tend to end up distracted. Naked and distracted.

"I'm not doing anything," he replies but when he speaks his breath tickles my neck and I get butterflies in my stomach. The butterflies get bigger as his lips curve into a smile where they're pressed against my neck, because the results are in. Two lines. Two very distinctive, no-doubt-about-it lines.

I spin around so we're facing each other and then we're both smiling and laughing and I wrap my legs around his waist as he carries me from the bathroom through to the adjoining master.

"You won't be able to do this much longer," I mumble.

"Do what? Make love to you in the middle of the day? The baby will nap, surely."

"No, silly. You won't be able to carry me like this much longer." My arms are on his shoulders with my fingers interwoven behind his neck. I look down at the gap between us and back at him. "I won't fit."

"Hmm, probably not." He drops me onto the bed with a dirty grin and I bounce as my ass hits the mattress. "I'll carry you sideways if need be. How's that?"

"You're supposed to say something more reassuring than that." I wrinkle my nose at him and narrow my eyes. "Lie to me. Tell me I'm going to gain less than a stone and total strangers will marvel over my svelte pregnancy figure."

I hear women at work talk about weight in terms of

246

stones. I've no idea what the conversion is to pounds but I like the idea of only needing to lose one of something.

I don't work for Jennings. I held firm on needing my own identity. It took months to find a job once I relocated to London and I was tempted to cave, to admit defeat and buckle to the fears that I'd be unable to find anything on my own. But I didn't. I stuck to it and eventually I found a position with a boutique design firm in London. I've learned so much and I love it and for now, it's a perfect fit.

Jennings still wants me to work for the family company, of course. He says I'm brilliant and I'm denying the company my talent. He fills my head with visions of walking to work together and secret afternoon trysts in his office.

I'll agree, someday. I've got a few more things I want to accomplish professionally on my own first. All in due time.

"Probably two or three stone," Jennings says. "I think you're more likely to gain two or three."

Oh. That's starting to sound like a lot. "But the baby will be a stone of that, right?"

"I should hope not, for your sake."

"That's not helpful." I really need to look into this stone thing more carefully.

"You're going to be the most gorgeously lush pregnant woman London has ever seen. Your pregnancy style will cause a sensation envied by women citywide, whilst every man under eighty will wish he were me."

"That's better."

I lie back on the bed as Jennings lies next to me, one hand spread across my flat stomach. Our heads are turned towards one another and I rest my hand on top of his. He's making the softest circles on my stomach, the touch a combination of possessive and comforting.

"You'll be stunning. I won't be able to keep my hands off of you."

"You won't?"

"I promise you I won't. I'm quite looking forward to watching your body change."

"You are?" This is news to me. He's made his interest in children clear, but without pressuring me. He respected my need to establish my career on a new continent and has patiently waited for me to be ready. We've talked about it in the abstract, checking in with each other on timing and interest, but this I've not heard.

"You'll be huge by summer and I'm going to buy you loads of pregnancy sundresses."

"How sweet. And I'll still love you when you have no hair." He's got great hair. It was all I could come up with.

He laughs. "It'll get me off. Seeing you swell with my child."

Damn. That's some caveman talk right there. And makes me a little excited, if I'm being honest.

"Are you proud of yourself?" I ask him, fighting the grin from my face and doing my best to ask the question innocently.

"For knocking you up?"

"Yes."

"Quite chuffed, yes."

I laugh then, giggling until something else occurs to me. "Wait." I bolt straight up on the bed and stare at Jennings. "I'm going to have a baby in England."

"Yes. That's indeed what's happening."

"Do you do it the same here?"

"Do what the same?"

"Deliver babies."

"I believe they do it the same everywhere, love."

"This country doesn't even know what Hidden Valley Ranch is. Nothing is the same."

"I'm not sure one has anything to do with the other, but I'll ensure a case of salad dressing is shipped over before your due date."

"People don't refrigerate their eggs here."

"Also not relevant, but we can go over that again if you like."

"This country doesn't celebrate Thanksgiving and no one eats pumpkin pie." I've hopped off the bed now to pace and I wave my hand at him about the pie.

"Violet, you don't like pumpkin pie."

"That's a valid point," I agree.

"We have afternoon tea in England. You know how you enjoy the mini-sandwiches and the assorted cakes."

"Also true, but what does that have to do with delivering a baby?"

"Nothing." He shakes his head. "I thought we were just talking gibberish about the differences between our homelands."

"No, babe. I have a point."

"Of course you do." He nods without laughing at me, which is a really important quality in a husband.

"What if I do it wrong? What if I go into labor and they say, 'Sorry, Violet, you were supposed to have pre-booked a room, you'll need to deliver it yourself now. Good luck?'"

"That's not likely to happen anywhere in the UK. Or elsewhere for that matter."

"You never know."

"Tell you what," Jennings says, sitting up on the bed and putting on his thinking face. It's the face he uses when he's trying to rationalize with me about things such as the lack of flavored coffee creamer available in this country.

"What?"

"We'll use the same hospital Will and Kate did. Will that work for you?"

"Shut up!" I gasp. I stop pacing and face him. "We can do that? For real? Normal people have babies there?" If they delivered the future king of England then they can probably deliver this kid.

"Yes. We can do that. Anyone willing to pay private hospital fees can do that. Is that the end of your concerns?"

"It is for now, but I reserve the right to change my mind at any time."

"Of course."

"Good thing we just finished the renovation on the mews house." That's what they call a guest house over here. A mews house. It was originally a carriage house— like an actual carriage house. For horse-drawn carriages. Insane, right? I can't believe I live in a house old enough that it has a horse garage.

I mean a mews house. Jennings has told me repeatedly that horse garage is not the correct term.

In any case it's renovated now, top to bottom. Two-car garage on the ground floor, a kitchen and living space above it and two guest bedrooms above that. Perfect for visiting family to stay as long as they like. Plus that's just the guest quarters. We've got more room in the main house, but don't get me started on that. No, really, don't. It took two years to renovate.

I loved every minute of it, of course.

Do you ever look up dream houses on the internet and imagine what it would be like to actually live in them? It's like that. Only better, because it's in London and the original details are a design dream come true. Imagine a historical townhouse on one of the best streets in Mayfair and an unlimited renovation budget. I could come just thinking about it and it's my house.

"Why is that a good thing? We'll be keeping the baby in the main house, surely." He grins when he says it so I know he's teasing.

We'll be keeping the baby in the nursery adjacent to the master bedroom. I might not have been ready for a baby when I drew up the plans for the remodel, but like any good designer, I planned for the future.

"My parents will want to stay when the baby comes. Plus my sister and her crew."

"Ah, yes. I look forward to it."

If I've one complaint about the British, it's that I'm not always certain when they're teasing. I side-eye Jennings now as I try to determine if he's sincere or not. And my sister—well, she does love to mention that Jennings fired her any chance she gets. But she's teasing. It's not like she'd have been able to go back anyway.

"Are you taking the piss out of me?" That's British for sarcasm. Taking the piss. It's not my favorite of the Britishisms but it doesn't stop me from using it whenever the opportunity arrives.

"Of course not, love. I'm attempting to get into your knickers."

"Oh. Well, in that case, carry on."

THE END

ACKNOWLEDGEMENTS

Whew! Another book done. "Done and dusted" as my friend Amy Jennings would say. It's one of her favorite phrases and it's fitting that I will start these acknowledgements with Amy. Thank you for letting me lift your last name for Jennings. For the rest of you, in case as you were reading thinking hmm, Jennings isn't the most usual name that's where I got it. Naming characters is honestly a lot harder and less fun than it looks. You end up with a page full of scribble and when you finally think you've come up with the perfect name you message your friend Kristi and say something like, "I really like the name Camden, I haven't used it yet right?" Three hours later you remember that you've already used Camden as a last name for a major character. #Fail

Anyway, Jennings. I'm picky about names. I don't normally like anything too different, but I do like last names as first names sometimes. And Jennings just fit. Once I thought of him as Jennings he couldn't have been anyone else.

So, this book. I first had the idea for this book three years ago—while I was writing Wrong and not expecting I'd ever write another book. I was on vacation—a Christmas Market tour in Germany, which by the way is my JAM. European Christmas Markets are MAGIC. Anyway, it was a guided tour, much like Violet was leading in Sure Thing. They're very popular in Europe—every place we stopped had large busses/coaches from multiple tour companies. They're not quite as big a thing in America, but they are available.

My mind instantly went to—what if the tour guide switched places with someone else? How would any of us know? How would the company even know? Because I'm me, I asked questions. "Hey, do you and the driver know each other? Or like, did you just meet?" Weirdo passenger, aisle 3. So that's where the idea was born. I can't remember if my initial thought was twins or if that came later, but that's where it started.

Thank you as always to my editor RJ Locksley & my formatter Erik Gevers for putting up with my up to the last second timelines. I appreciate you both!!! Thanks to Marion Making Manuscripts and Karen Lawson for your early read and feedback.

Kari March—I don't think thank you is big enough, but thank you for putting up with me and helping me get this cover just right. And not blocking my email from ever contacting you again.

Jade West, you have no idea how much your support and asking for more chapters meant to me. For listening to me obsess over what the next chapter should be. You were a total rock star for me on this book.

Franzi, Jean, Kristi, Bev, Michelle thank you for reading & encouraging.

So now you want to know, what's next?

Well, there's Daisy. I think we all deserve to know exactly what she was up to when she dumped the tour on Violet and took off. She had a very good reason, I promise. I envision this "series" as just the two books, one for Violet and one for Daisy.

Then there's Rhys and Canon. And some other guys I haven't introduced yet. I envision the Vegas series as a minimum of two books and a maximum of who knows. I'm imagining a whole lot of fun & debauchery with a bunch of bachelors living in a hotel. These books will be interconnected stand alones about different couples.

Finally, dear reader, thank YOU. I honestly can't believe I'm a writer. I still sorta shrug when people ask me what I do and then I answer like I'm uncertain. "Um, I'm a writer?" Then they reply something like, "oh, that's nice," and I'll say something really chatty like, "yeah." It's your support that allows me to be awkward with strangers about my career, and more importantly, it keeps me in my pajamas where I belong. Sipping on a steady stream of iced coffee that I've procured from the Starbucks drive-thru, while still in my pajama's.

XO, Jana

SOCIAL MEDIA

I have a reader group on Facebook so if you're into that sort of thing, please join us at Grind Me Café

Follow me on Social Media
Facebook: Jana Aston
Twitter: @janaaston
Website: Janaaston.com
Instagram: janaaston

If you prefer to avoid social media and have my release news sent right to your mailbox, sign up for my newsletter at
app.mailerlite.com/webforms/landing/y8g3v8

ALSO BY JANA ASTON

The Wrong Series:
WRONG

RIGHT

FLING

TRUST

Standalone:
Times Square

ABOUT THE AUTHOR

Jana Aston likes cats, big coffee cups and books about billionaires who deflower virgins. She wrote her debut novel while fielding customer service calls about electrical bills, and she's ever grateful for the fictional gynecologist in Wrong that readers embraced so much she was able to make working in her pajamas a reality.

Jana's work has appeared on the NYT, WSJ and USA Today bestsellers lists, some multiple times. She likes multiples.

CPSIA information can be obtained
at www.ICGtesting.com
Printed in the USA
LVHW112147270521
688760LV00014B/351